Grand Canyon Rescue:

A Tuli Black Wolf Adventure

Booklocker.com, Inc.
2004

Grand Canyon Rescue:

A Tuli Black Wolf Adventure

Devon Mihesuah

To my son Toshaway with hopes that he always will be a
conscientious and safe outdoorsman

Table of Contents

Chapter 1: I'm Not Really Lost

"Oh, no," cried Mr. Wabash, the biggest of the three men. "We're gonna stay out here until we die.

Mr. Wabash has tattoos on his hairy neck, which probably means he put tattoos on his arms. Both ears are pierced. His hair is tied back in a ponytail, but it doesn't look like he brushed it first. How come people think if they pull their hair back they don't have to brush it? Even that cowboy hat can't cover up his messy hair.

"I never thought the trip would end up like this," Mr. Johnston said. He was much quieter, smaller and less hairy than his friend Mr. Wabash. He had tears in his eyes and I thought he might cry, too.

Jody Johnston, whose father is also named Jody, is around 15. Yesterday he fell and sliced his lip, leaving blood all over his shirt. Now his mouth is swollen and he hurts. He doesn't say much, mainly because his lip is too puffy.

"L-l-look, if any of you get out of here t-t-tell my wife and kids I love them," said Mr. Martin in his quiet, stuttering voice that sounds like he's missing some vocal cords. He's even bigger than Mr. Wabash. His belly is large and his heavy moustache hangs down past the corners of his mouth. It looks like one of those scrub brushes Mom uses to clean the floor. He still looks pretty cool though, because he wears the same sunglasses the Terminator wore in his first movie.

I hardly ever see men cry. My little brother is five and he cries a lot. But adults are different. Mom tells me that men are afraid to let the tears flow. They act like people will think they're babies if they get caught crying.

All three men and young Jody are dressed in camouflage clothes and boots. Each one has a rifle, hunting knife on their belt

1

and a full pack. If they're so well-outfitted, how come they're lost in the middle of the North Rim of the Grand Canyon?

Mom can answer the question about why people get lost better than anyone. She teaches third grade for a living. But what she's really good at is finding lost people. She volunteers for the McAlester Search and Rescue Dog Association (SRDA) that is part of the National Association for Search and Rescue. The group is small, with just Mom, four other handlers and their twelve dogs. Four of the dogs are puppies.

Because Mom is good at what she does she's asked to travel across the country to assist in rescues. Usually she has to leave fast after a phone call. That's why her search backpacks are in the mud room ready for her to grab as she runs out the door to meet the helicopter or airplane.

My mom knows about the minds of lost people and says that appearances aren't everything.

"Just because you have the right equipment doesn't mean you know what to do with it," Mom says. "Hunters and hikers with big packs crammed with food, clothes, even maps and compass get lost every season in almost every state in the country. The number of people who have no pack and get lost is even higher."

Then she'd look at me and my brother. "And don't you ever even think about getting lost. You should know better. "*Hash imponna*," she says in Choctaw, which means "you are smart."

Mom is always telling me and my brother Pete about how to stay alive if we lose our way outdoors. We talk about survival a lot, especially on week-ends when we take long hikes. Mom makes us name plants and animals and then she gives lessons in orienteering. That's using a map and compass to find your way from one place to another.

Even if I have a map and compass Mom still tells me, "Stay put when you first think you're lost, honey. The more you wander around the harder it is for trackers to find you."

I thought that everyone knew that, although it's pretty clear that the hunters I'm stuck with never took a survival course.

No one in my family has ever been lost. My dad isn't a tracker, but he always knows where he is. He's a vet who specializes in big animals, like horses and cows. The fun part is that he gets to work for zoos since he knows a lot about elephant, tiger and bear digestive systems.

The knowledge Dad learned for his job is not real helpful if he's out in the wilderness, but he's useful to take along on camping trips and hikes because he can identify the animal bones we find. Between what Dad and Mom teach me, I know a lot about animals, their tracks and what their bones look like.

Our house in Oklahoma is in the woods by a stream and lots of wildlife. I know to tell people where I'm going before hiking through the fields and woods around us. I've taken CPR, first aid classes and am an advanced swimmer. I can identify trees, insects, plants and know what is poisonous. I like getting ready for having problems in the wilderness. My packs are filled with gear to keep me warm and dry. I know how to track. Not as good as Mom, but I can follow deer until I find them.

She's told me that I read a map and compass slower than her, but just as accurately. I know where the constellations sit in the night sky as they wander through the seasons. I may be prepared for an outdoor problem, but I never thought I'd have to use that information to keep myself or anyone else alive.

"How long can we live without food?" Mr. Wabash asked in-between hiccups. The kind of hiccups you get after a good, hard cry.

I think crying is good for you and I do it lot. Of course, I'm a girl and I'm only 14.

Chapter 2: Hapi chumpuli and John

"*Ofi achukma*, John," I gasped. "You're a good dog too, Happy."

I talked to my dogs as we ran down the dusty dirt road. They trotted easily in front of me, the leashes pulling hard on my wrist. Sweat ran down my forehead and into my eyes. If I wiped it away I'd knock off my sunglasses, so I tried to ignore the salt sting.

Happy stopped suddenly to poop and I nearly fell when the leash yanked my arm. At least I got to take a quick breather. Having taken care of business, Happy took off even faster than before.

Mom said I could take one of her rescue dogs out for a run because the end of summer drew closer and that signaled the start of school. The hot, muggy August mornings also meant *kapucha* training was around the corner.

Kapucha, of course, is the traditional Choctaw stickball game that many members of the tribe still play, although over time it also grew into what is known as lacrosse in other parts of the country. I normally play *kapucha* year round with other Choctaws who are determined to keep our traditions alive. But this year was different. I hadn't played in months and had to get in shape fast.

That wouldn't be easy because I broke my leg in June after falling out of a tree looking for cicada shells. I had climbed twelve feet up one of our big pecan trees then reached for a shell with my right hand. My left hand held onto a thin branch. As I gently pulled the crispy brown cicada shell off the bark, my left hand slipped and I crashed through the branches to the ground.

Like cats often do, I landed on my feet, but the force of the fall caused my big bone, the tibia, to break below my knee. For eight frustrating weeks I hobbled around in a cast made of lime-green plaster. What felt worse was my leg had to stay straight.

More than anything I wanted to sit with my knee bent, tucked under my chin.

I hadn't run more than three miles since my cast came off two weeks ago. It took almost that long to break the adhesions around my joints and muscles so I could bend my knee and sit like a normal person. My stride looked and felt weird. And that was a big problem.

"If I'm going to play *kapucha*," I had told my mother that morning, "then I have to run more miles. And I have to run them a lot faster than I ran today."

"You're pushing it, Tuli. Just go two miles right now. You can take one dog," she told me.

When Mom said I could take a dog, she meant one dog. Not two. Mainly because two dogs are hard to handle when they want to run. But I was determined and willing to take a chance that Mom might not find out. I planned on making myself run until I got fit again. Even if that meant being dragged along the road by John and Happy.

"And I know you're upset at what happened the last game," Mom said after I came home from the hospital with a huge cast on my leg. "But you have to forget it, honey."

I guess I neglected to mention that during the last *kapucha* game I not only dropped the ball after an easy pass and didn't score, I got a side cramp and had to stop running. A couple of my friends hadn't talked to me all summer, even after I broke my leg. Having Arnie Anapatubbee and Jen Wilson ignore me was worse than anything that had ever happened in my life.

"It's not as if they played perfectly, honey," Mom said. "Jen tripped and fell twice during that game and Arnie hit another player across the face with her stick and broke her nose."

Still, I spent the entire month of June crying and not because my leg hurt. I felt like a fool.

Dad had another way of looking at it: "If you won at every time you played a game or ran a race Tuli, you'd never learn anything. And if you never make a mistake, then you'll always expect to win. And then when you fail, you'll never recover. Get used to losing, kid, because that's the way life is."

"But my friends, Dad," I cried.

"Tuli," Dad said in his soothing and smart voice, "Indians shouldn't be mad at each other, especially over a game. We have enough to deal with. Your little girl friends need to grow up. Do your best and everything will be all right." Then he kissed my forehead and said he'd get me get a Popsicle.

My dad is probably right. Still, knowing that I messed up the game for my team will continue to hurt my feelings until I can win again. At least that's what I convinced myself is true.

One way to win is to be fit. So, I was up at six o'clock in the morning along with the birds and insects that were already were flying around. The dogs spotted a squirrel and I could tell that John's little pea brain thought about chasing it.

"John! No!" I yelled quickly so I wouldn't be dragged off the road and into the brush.

Bugs buzzed and zig-zagged through the air as if they'd eaten too much sugar. I tried to reach where a mosquito sucked on the hard-to-scratch place above my elbow.

I love summer, but felt hot, sore and ready to sit in front of the air cooler. Happy and John pulled harder on their leashes, expecting a snack when we arrived at the house. When we almost reached the road that turned off to my home I looked up.

"*Halito Humma*-Hello Red," I gasped. The red-tailed hawk watches me from his perch on the top of his favorite telephone pole. Our neighbors grow a variety of crops on their farms and Red sits on the post looking for mice that run around in the alfalfa field below him.

Once, about a year ago, a perfect wing feather dropped from where Red sat. I wondered if he gave the feather to me or if his pretty speckled brown and red feather was old and the time had come to shed it. Mom said to consider the feather a gift so I told Red "*Hoshinko-vt achukma hoke. Yokoke.*" The hawk couldn't understand me, but I thanked her anyway for the beautiful feather.

"*Hoke*, John. *Hoke*, Happy," I said to my running partners, "Let's get home." In case you're wondering, the Choctaw word *hoke* is the same as the English word okay. In fact, that's where 'okay' came from.

Now before you think I'm talking about two boy dogs, I should say that both are females. John is a four-year-old German Short Haired Pointer with mainly brown coloring and big beige spots. Happy is a black five-year-old German Shepherd dog. I add the dog on there because the American Kennel Club does. Maybe that's because some people think a German Shepherd is a German sheepherder person.

The name Happy comes from my little brother not being able to say *hapi chumpuli*. That means 'sugar' in Choctaw. Johns name story isn't as interesting. She's named after my grandfather who gave her to my mother.

As we ran through the driveway gates I let go of the leashes. The dogs headed straight to their water buckets that stayed cool in shade from the red bud trees. Happy put her head in the 20-gallon metal container and lapped the water. John got in her bucket back legs first then sat in the water. John always acts determined to get in there and cool her body which meant I had to dump the dirty water out and refill it. I closed the gate behind me then walked slowly to the water faucet.

I only limped a little now, but knew I'd limp badly after my shower. My two bags of frozen peas waited for me in the freezer. That's the best kind of cold pack to put on a sore body part because you can mold it to fit your knee, ankle, wrist, forehead or whatever hurts you. I turned on the hose and held the nozzle over my head while the cool water ran down my face and into my ears. I felt a nice chill as the water made its way down my neck and back.

My brother Pete came out onto the back porch. A lot of little kids like to sleep late when they don't have to go to school. Not Pete. He always wakes up early. This morning he held an orange juice pop in one hand and scratched his head with the other. His dark hair stood up on top and stuck out on the sides. We have the same dark eyes and thick brown hair although his is short. But his eyelashes are so long they look fake. How come some guys look like they wear mascara and us girls put on makeup and use an eyelash curler?

"*Halito antek*-Hello Sister. How far did ya go?" Pete asked. Juice ran down his chin and onto the stop watch that hung around his neck.

"About four miles."

"That's too far right now, Tuli." Pete sounds a lot older than a five year old. "Your leg can't handle it. Plus you didn't go very fast. I timed you. Slower than yesterday."

"Thanks for telling me." I took off my water-filled shoes and as I limped past Pete, I grabbed the waist band of his Sponge Bob undies and gave him a wedgie.

"Mom!" he yelled as I headed for the shower.

I stood under the warm spray until I felt clean then turned the knob with the blue X in the middle so I'd get a cold blast to help me stop sweating. Then I wiped off the steamed-up mirror to see my brown skin looking like I had on pink blush. I get so hot while running that my face flushes. After dressing in my favorite cut-offs and black t-shirt I walked to the den water cooler. The moist air blowing on my face felt wonderful.

"How was your run, honey?" Mom asked. She had dressed in her running shorts and t-shirt and waited for me to return. It was my turn to watch Pete while she went out for a few miles. I like that my parents do the same things I do. Except that she does everything better and it makes me mad sometimes. She can beat me at running and swimming and she knows the answers on "Jeopardy."

"Pretty good," I told her. "My knee hurts a little."

"I'm not surprised." She rubbed sun screen on her cheeks and nose that always looked tan. "You didn't bend your knee for two months. That heavy cast made you lopsided and now both your legs have to recover. You gimped around off-kilter for quite a while, you know."

She braided her long pony tail and as she tied the end with a band, she looked down at me. "How far did you go?" she asked.

"Four miles," I said quietly.

"Tuli." Mom said evenly. She doesn't have to yell to sound mad.

"Told ya she was going too far," Pete said from the kitchen doorway. He finished his juice pop and now crunched on an apple slice smeared with peanut butter.

Before she could lecture me I jumped in. "Mom, I gotta get in shape. I'm not gonna be a good player. I'm . . ."

"Tulip Louise," she said again. "Your leg isn't healed enough to run that far. You only should be walking maybe one or two miles."

"Two miles!" I blurted out.

Mom held up a hand for me to be quiet. "You're limping and that's going to make your back hurt. Then your neck will hurt. Remember that your body parts are all connected and one injury affects all of you. You're pushing too hard."

"But *kapucha*," I whined.

"Honey," she said as she walked over to me. She put her sunglasses on her head and knelt on her knees so she could look into my eyes. Mom's pretty tall. "We talked about this. You may not be able to play your best on the team this year. It's not the end of the world, honey. You can play *kapucha* the rest of your life. Maybe you could run cross country instead. There isn't as much twisting and turning."

I felt the tears building. I wanted to play *kapucha* more than almost anything.

She stood and put on her sunglasses then her cap that has CHOCTAW NATION embroidered on it with bright thread. "You have to rebuild those muscles slowly."

"Mom," Pete said. "Can I have a banana?"

"Yes sweetie, you can. Aren't you full yet?"

Pete looked down his nose at his belly as if he could see through to his stomach. "I don't think so."

His full tummy stuck out like a little basketball. He likes vegetables and fruit and yoghurt, so at least he's full of good things. We like the same foods, but if I ate as much as Pete I wouldn't fit through the door. Dad says I'm skinny and Mom says not to forget my morning vitamin.

"Being fit is more important than looking like a model, honey," Mom always tells me. "Eating fresh foods and exercising makes you healthy and thin. If you just eat junk like French Fries, soda and candy, you'll end up old, big and sick." Since I don't get sick and always feel good, so there has to be something to that advice.

Mom walked to the door and gazed out the screen to where the dogs splashed in their water. She put her hand on the door handle. "There's oatmeal in the pot. Heat it up in the microwave. Blueberries are in the fridge and brown sugars on the table. Drink some water or else you'll get a headache. And don't turn on that television."

She left without another word. I went to the window and watched Mom close the gate behind her. Then she ran easily down the road, her waist-length black hair streaked with gray flowing behind her. My hair is just as long, but I like to twirl it into a bun and fasten it with a big butterfly clip so the sweaty strands don't get on my neck.

Dang, I said to myself. So much for watching the Sci Fi channel. Mom and Dad want me and Pete to read books and wildlife magazines instead of flipping channels. They think that building our minds and bodies are the most important goals we can have.

Mom also says that because I'm a girl and an Indian that I better get off my rear, get smart and make myself happy.

"There always will be people ready to make you feel bad, honey," she told me. "Indians have to deal with stereotypes and racism every day. People think we're not smart, that we're drunks and on welfare. Some think we talk to animals and cry when we see litter."

Well, that's sure true. Kids in my class ask me weird questions like, 'Do you live in a tipi?' 'Where's your horse?' "Dances With Wolves" may have made some people more aware of the culture of one Plains tribe in the late 1800s, but it sure doesn't help us modern-day Indians who originally lived in Mississippi.

One time a lady at the gas station called Mom a 'squaw,' which is about the worse thing you can say to her. Pete and I were in the car and we watched as Mom's face turned red and she clinched her fists.

Instead of tearing into that woman with a bunch of curse words, Mom calmly said, "At least I have enough pride in myself not to call other people names. And I'm so sorry that someone styled your hair that way when you were sleeping. You must be mortified." Then she rattled off a string of Choctaw that I didn't understand, although I caught a few words like *ikaiuklo*, which means 'ugly' and *imanukfila iksho* which means 'stupid.' Afterwards Mom got in the car and stayed quiet all the way home.

I thought about that incident a lot. Mom says we should never call other people names, but maybe she meant you could call them names in Choctaw? Anyway, Mom also says we have to have pride in ourselves and the best way to do that is to learn our history, our language and to work to make our Choctaw Nation strong. She pushes herself to be the best she can be. And she always stands up for herself. She exercises hard, looks for better ways to teach her students, and she's known as one of the best search and rescue trackers in the country. Last year PEOPLE magazine did an article about her and the fact that she always finds her man. Using dogs just makes the process go quicker.

Mom expected me to try as hard as she does. With school, with positive thinking, with speaking up, when people talk badly about Natives. From what I could tell, Mom didn't fail. As I thought about how hard it must be for her to live up to the standards she makes for herself, I looked out the window at her long, fast stride until she got to the green alfalfa field where she turned the corner and disappeared.

Chapter 3: What Happened on the Rim

On Halloween, the thirty-first day of October in Unit 12A, which is the North Rim of the Grand Canyon in the Kaibab National Forest, the wives of three hunters reported that their husbands did not call them by midnight. They were to have finished their hunt that day and should have called them from the lodge at Jacob's Lake before dark. The hunters live in Phoenix and this was their first hunting trip.

The Sheriff's posse in Northern Arizona thought they'd find the hunters themselves that night. Well, they didn't, which is why our Sheriff called Mom the next morning.

Dad left early to help a rancher deliver a foal. Pete and I got dressed for school and snacked on fat blueberries while we watched Mom stir oatmeal in one pot and grits in another.

"*Himmak nitak achukma*-It's a nice day," Mom said as she looked out the kitchen window. She tries to teach us Choctaw and figures that meal times are the best times. That's because we can't go anywhere, we have to listen in order to get fed, and there's a lot of food and silverware words to learn.

"*Nanta ikbi-li o?*-What am I making?" She asked us.

"Uh," Petie stammered. "*Onnahinli impa*-Breakfast."

"Yes, dear. But *what* am I making?"

"*Yansh lakchi?*-Grits?"

Mom, Dad and I prefer oatmeal while Pete likes grits with a variety of stuff in it. On week-ends Mom makes him cheese and jalapeno grits that you can slice like brownies after the pan sets in the refrigerator.

"And?"

"*Isuba apa*-Oats?"

"Good. And what are you drinking, Tuli?"

"*Pishukchi kapvssa*-Cold milk." I knew that for sure because I'd said it about a thousand times already.

And we went on like that, with Mom asking us to name basic stuff like knife, fork, spoon and water, then we'd answer *bashpo, chufak, isht impa, oka.*

"You need to learn as much of our language as you can," she'd tell us. "Your language is who you are."

"Mom," I'd argue, "if there isn't anyone to talk to in Choctaw besides us and relatives when we go visit them, then why do we need to know *Chahta anumpa?*"

Mom would sigh and answer, "Because if you lose the language you lose your identity. You're both doing well in school right now, so in the spring I want you to take Lillie Robert's *Chahta anumpa* grammar course on the web. It's Tuesday and Thursday nights."

"Shawn speaks Cherokee," Pete said. Shawn Adair being the 14 year-old guy in my eighth grade class who started calling me last month. He's a half-blood Cherokee from Tahlequah whose family moved to McAlester in August. We get along fine because he runs cross country and is Indian, too. He asked me to the high school football game this Friday and I was excited about it, even if his parents were going along.

"That's right," Mom said. "He knows his language and you should too." That was only one reason Mom liked him. Shawn's smart, cute and runs fast.

"Yeah, I know Mom."

"Don't worry, Tuli,' Pete said in his sympathetic voice. "Shawn doesn't know all the words."

"Okay," Mom said with a smile. "Enough. Now, let's talk about early winter."

The phone rang in the middle of Mom's lesson about why some Choctaws still refer to November as *Hochafo chito*: big hunger month. It has to do with the history of our tribe. Long ago, before the time of grocery stores, much of the food harvested from summer crops had started to disappear by November. So, people started to get really hungry.

Mom looked at the "caller id" attached to the answering machine. "Sheriff," she told us.

"Oh boy," said Pete. He looked excited. "We need some action around here."

"Don't hope for too much, son," Mom said.

Mom hit the 'intercom' button and talked while she cooked. "Hey Gin," the deep voice said on the speaker phone.

"Lincoln, how are you?" Mom asked Lincoln Murray, Sheriff of McAlester.

"I'm okay. They got a situation in Arizona and need you out there."

"Arizona? Where abouts?"

"Grand Canyon."

"The Canyon?" Mom laughed even though I knew she didn't think what he said was funny. "Man, that is a problem."

"Well, the North Rim. It's not inside the Canyon. The Rim's above 7000 feet and is at least 30 degrees cooler in the summer than it is down by the Colorado River. A lot colder in winter, too. Anyway, looks like an early snow storm is coming in and we got three hunters who didn't call home when they were supposed to. They have a kid with them. The son of one of the hunters. Actually, the kid is one of the hunters. Kid and father both got drawn. You know how hard it is to get drawn for hunting deer on the North Rim?"

"Nope," said Mom. "I don't hunt."

She took the pan of grits off the fire and poured a small bowl for Pete, who promptly poured in raisins, brown sugar and a glob of 'I Can't Believe It's Not Butter.'

"Forest Service guys found their vehicle," Sheriff Murray continued, "but the Ford truck had three cell phones in it. The three wives gave the Sheriff their cell numbers. Some guys riding

ATVs found their camp site off Road 252 in case you have a map there. It's a bit south of Big Springs."

"No map of the North Rim here," Mom said.

"No matter. You can get one en route."

"So they didn't take their cell phones into the field?"

"Looks like they didn't."

"Pretty dumb," Pete commented as he slurped his bowl of grits.

"Pete," she said. "No name-calling, please."

"Cell phones don't work up there," Lincoln said.

"Not calling in isn't so unusual, anyway," Mom said to the speaker phone. "If one or more of the hunters got a deer and had trouble dressing it they might be out working on it a long time."

Dressing a deer means to take off the skin, then remove the innards, head and all that. See, some hunters can shoot pretty well, but have all kinds of trouble getting their prey skinned. Sometimes they take all night if they shoot a deer in the evening.

Mom turned off the fire under the oatmeal and added skim milk, sunflower seeds, raisins and wheat germ to the pot of mush. She spooned a bowl for her and one for me. She allowed me to put in two spoons of white sugar while she preferred a pack of Sweet 'n Low and a bit of brown sugar.

"Doubtful they got a deer," Sheriff Murray said. "They've never hunted before. You ever go huntin'?"

"No." Mom hasn't a hunter and she had no interest in hunting, but she sure can shoot a rifle and bow. And she can get so close to deer that once she shot a photograph of a buck's just-shed antler falling to the ground. But the shot that really gets everyone's attention is the one of a mountain lion's back legs and tail. She actually had tracked the lion and followed behind it without the animal ever realizing she was there.

Mom took a bite of hot oatmeal and thought a few seconds before speaking loudly towards the phone. "No walkie talkies?"

"No m'am."

"That means they aren't ready to be lost."

"I'd bet on that," the Sheriff agreed. "Nothing like an unprepared hunter lost in tough country with a storm coming. One other thing, they're at altitude. If they aren't used to thin air they'll be more tired than usual."

Pete looked at me. "What's altitude?" he whispered.

Since I had just studied that in school last spring, I could tell him. "Altitude is well, how far you are above sea level. We're pretty much at sea level. The higher up you go, the less oxygen there is. That's why people who climb high mountains like Everest usually take oxygen bottles. You can get altitude sickness if you're not used to the mountains. You can get real tired. We got sick last summer in the Rockies, remember?"

"Oh yeah, you puked."

"So did you."

"Hush," Mom stared at us.

"What?" Asked Sheriff Murray.

"Not you, Lincoln. My kids."

Pete smiled as he ate. He got his answer and was satisfied.

"I hope they got enough water and warm clothes," Lincoln said. "It's getting' real cold at night on the Rim. It was 20 degrees last night and now a front's moving in. It's gonna rain and maybe snow."

Mom and Dad tell me to be prepared. Even on short hikes I always take my fanny pack that holds everything I need. And I never put myself in a situation where I can get lost.

The only times I go out by myself are road runs and Mom knows exactly when to expect me back home. She's come after me with the truck more than a few times because I didn't come back when I said I would.

"They're in a world of trouble already," Mom said.

"Gin, the helicopter will be at the airport in forty minutes. Can you make it?"

"I'll be there," she said. "But two members of my unit are out of town. The only ones who can go are me and Rowdy." She meant George "Rowdy" Willard and his two German Shepherds.

"That'll have to do."

"Isn't there a Unit in Northern Arizona?" She asked.

"Yeah, but the Flagstaff team is looking for a lost kid around Lake Mary."

"Where's the Albuquerque unit? Why can't they go?"

"They're with the Dallas unit in the Colorado Rockies range trying to find a downed Cessna airplane."

"That should be easy to find," Pete said.

"Not really," Mom said. "Lots of times a plane hits the ground hard. It breaks apart and the prices are scattered. Sometimes the whole plane jams into the ground and you can't see it from above because leaves and branches cover it."

"But the dogs can find it."

"Sometimes. But every now and then planes crash after flying so off course that they stay lost for weeks and even months. It takes a long time and lots of money to search even small areas. Not even dogs can help if no one knows where the plane went down."

I thought about Sheriff Murray's call to Mom. There aren't that many canine search and rescue units that specialize in wilderness work. Many times units have to cross state lines. And country lines. Mom went to India a few years ago to look for earthquake victims and then to Alaska to find bodies after an avalanche. Happy isn't trained as a cadaver dog but still, she's good at finding bodies in the snow. Mom says it's a gift Happy has.

"Okay, Lincoln," Mom said. "Gotta get ready. Bye." She pressed the intercom button, then speed-dialed another number.

After a few rings, Dad picked up his cell phone. "Lo?"

"Hi Hon," Mom greeted him. "Busy?"

"Just delivered the foal. The kids would love it."

"Hi Dad!" yelled Pete.

"Hi Petie. What's up?" He asked.

"Just got a call from Lincoln." Mom gathered dishes and put them in the sink as she spoke. "I have to go to the Grand Canyon to find some hunters."

"When?" I heard a clang in the background. Dad had dropped something metal into a pan.

"Few minutes. The helicopter's at the airport. I'm taking Tuli."

"What?" I said loudly. I was surprised. Usually I only get to go on searches close to our house. Like when we look for tornado victims and I don't like doing that because the victims are never lost. They're dead.

"What about school?" Dad asked.

"I'll call in for her and she can get her assignments when we come back. I think this is important for her to do. I have to call in and tell them I'll need a sub."

"Okay. Hopefully you won't be gone more than a few days. I'll be at the office a while this morning. A dog with a dislocated hip is coming in. I'll pick Pete up this afternoon. Call Oscar and see if he can watch him for a while before school."

"Oh boy," said Pete.

Oscar is my dad's friend who's a little older than my parents. He owns a bike shop in town, dances in pow wows and makes a lot of money doing it. He also has an animal rehabilitation center just a few blocks away from us and takes care of birds of prey and small mammals like foxes, opossums and raccoons that get hit by cars. We visit on the weekends and help take care of the animals.

"Great idea. He'd love it." Mom smiled and winked at Pete, who'd given her the thumbs up. "Gotta move fast now, hon. Love you. I'll call later."

"Be careful, Gin," Dad said. "You too, Tuli. Don't get lost."

Mom hung up then called Oscar and my school to say that I'd be absent.

I sat there shocked and happy that Mom said she'd take me and then I remembered: the football game.

"Mom, the game's on Friday."

"So?"

"You think there won't be other games? I promise he'll understand. Call and tell him. You know his number?"

Well, I wasn't going to admit that I had memorized it. I paused until Mom looked the other way then punched in Shawn's number with a shaking finger. Pete put his hand on my arm and that made me feel better. I left a message on his recorder that I hoped make sense: "Hi Shawn. This is uh, Tuli and uh, well, I may not be able to go to the game Friday because well, I have to go search for some lost hunters with my mom at the North Rim of the Grand Canyon. It's just Tuesday, but we don't know how long it'll take. If I get back in time I'll call you. Okay? Bye."

Did that make sense? I sure wasn't going to call back and make my message any clearer.

"Tuli," she yelled from down the hall. I hurried to see if I could help her get ready. "Get your gear. Add your winter bag to it."

Knowing my Mom, it would only take her a minute to dress in her search gear, that is, heavy hunting pants, a long-sleeved denim shirt over polypropylene long underwear, heavy socks and light hiking boots that she could run in, just in case she needed to run. She already had packed her heavier snow boots in the large pack a month before.

"Wait," she shouted. "Feed the dogs first and tell Pete to pull their gear bag into the kitchen."

I headed out the door. "And get some extra garbage bags and your gaiters," she yelled after me. "It might snow. Tell Pete to make some peanut butter and jelly sandwiches for us."

I gave John and Happy a light breakfast of Pro Plan, Brewer's Yeast and warm water, then ran back inside to grab my gear bag that I always keep packed. A smaller bag that also contains some foul weather gear always sits next to the main camp bag that bulges with our tent, tarps and cook gear. I had room to spare in the smaller pack so I folded extra winter pants, tops, hats, gloves and stuff like that into it. Then I dressed in the same kind of clothes as Mom.

I returned to the kitchen where I quickly ate my bowl of oatmeal and raisins while Mom brushed and braided my long hair. As Pete ate his pear, the juice ran down his chin.

"You're gonna pop, brother," I told him.

"Nope. I'm like a balloon. I just keep growing."

"Balloons pop."

"Nope. I just get gas." He laughed loud like he had made a great joke.

"Did you make the sandwiches and get the dogs' bag, son?" Mom asked Pete in that breathless voice she gets when she's in a hurry.

Pete had a mouth crowded full of pear so he gave the thumbs up again then pointed to the counter. Three sandwiches in baggies lay neatly stacked next to the blender and the dog's bag lay on the floor.

"Good boy," Mom said. She often spoke to us in the same way she speaks to the dogs. "One more thing, Sweetie Petie. Check the camp bag for utensils. Dad may have taken them out.

We're probably gonna have to set up our own camp."

That meant we'd have to take our tents and cook ware. Most search operations include local volunteers who bring food. But if there weren't any cooks on this trip, things would get mighty uncomfortable way out on the North Rim without adequate supplies. Mom always insists on taking our own food and equipment. Just in case.

"Okay, we gotta get to the helicopter in 20 minutes. You mind Oscar, Pete. He'll get you to school today. Daddy will pick you up."

We heard a knock at the door and Pete ran to answer. "Oscar!" He yelled.

In walked a short, dark man wearing a cowboy hat, v-neck blue sweater, jeans and boots. His right hand held a thermos while the other carried a sack containing something heavy.

"What is it? What is it? What is it?" Pete piped like a baby bird desperate for a worm.

"Well let's see now," Oscar said in his booming voice.

He pulled out a book with a colorful cover and said, "Looks like a book on tying knots."

"Yipee," Pete shrieked as he grabbed the treasure and ran down the hall with it.

"And what else do we have?" Oscar asked as he looked into his bag. "Looks like a water bottle."

"Oh, wow," I managed to say. I mean, a water bottle? How excited can you get about that?

He pulled out a bottle with a soft wrap around it and a handle. "See here," he showed me. "You put your hand through the loop and grip the bottle like this and you can't drop it. And it has a zipper on the side for keys. You change out the bottle when it gets cracked or gets too much bacteria in it."

"Oh." That was more like it. I took my present and put my hand around it. "Cool. Thanks."

"I have a young opossum in the car. I need to feed her every hour. Okay if I do it here?"

"Of course," Mom said. "But you'll have a heck of time getting Pete to school once he sees it."

That's for sure. We both go nuts over animals that Oscar lets us feed.

"Tuli," Mom urged. "We have to hurry." Mom finished my hair and went to the fridge. "Get yourself some snacks. Put some of those breakfast bars and V8s in the lunch bag. Plus some Motrin packets, beef jerky and the dried apricots we bought last week that no one ate. They'll be nice and dry by now," she added sarcastically.

Sometimes travel takes longer than my stomach can handle. I'm pretty much hungry all the time and there are few things more uncomfortable than being hungry on a trip and not having a thing to eat.

What's worse is being lost without food or water. I'd always hoped not to find myself in that situation. But I also thought it would be cool to find out what being lost feels like. As long as I wouldn't really starve or get hurt.

Mom always says, "Don't hope for too much, Tuli. You might get what you hope for and that may be more than you want." Boy, was she ever right about that.

Chapter 4: In the Choppers

"John, *chulosa*-hush up," Mom said as she drove us to the airport where we met the helicopter. John knew she was going to work. So we had the honor of listening to her whine with excitement the whole way.

I rummaged through my fanny pack for some Dramamine. I felt queasy just thinking about the trip. Whenever Mom flies on a plane she brings home some of those wax-lined throw-up bags they stow in the seat backs. Barf bags are handy during our family trips when we ride over washboard roads to remote camping sites. I get sick on long trips and my brother can throw up just going over a speed bump.

I looked some more. Darn. No Dramamine. Well, luckily I didn't eat a big breakfast.

Mom has done this hurrying-to-the-airport routine many times and knew she could scoot right up to the 'copter. We parked in a covered space then unloaded the gear and the animals. Both dogs sat on the tarmac and waited. Happy looked happy, her tongue out and her eyes bright. John continued to whine like a baby, only now because her nervous side had kicked in. The dogs have been in helicopters before and only one of them likes the ride.

The pilot jogged over and took our packs. "Your friend is over there," he said, pointing to the tall man who stood between the big plane and one of those caterpillar carts that carry luggage. As soon as the cart moved we saw that Rowdy's two dogs were on leashes attached to his wrist. His two packs sat on the ground.

Rowdy wore clothes similar to me and Mom. "Let's go," Mom said. I took Happy while Mom held on to John. We carried our heavy packs.

Mom's search and rescue friend Rowdy was a bit older than her, if you go by how a person looks. He'd been in the group for five years. His two dogs, Barney and Cosmo, are big German Shepherds who had also done police work. That meant I wasn't supposed to approach them by myself because they had also been trained to attack if need be.

I never had problems with either of them. Both put their paws up to shake my hand and both liked to lick my face. Mom, however, gets nervous around them. "What if you make a sudden movement they think is aggressive?" She'd ask me. Mom tends to be overprotective and is leery of police dogs. They like her too, but she keeps one eye on them when kids are around.

Rowdy gave me a hug and patted John and Happy. All the dogs touched noses and smelled butts.

"Looks like it's just us," Mom said. "Darren and Cindy are out of town early for Thanksgiving."

"We can handle it," Rowdy answered.

"I hope so. I'm not good in cold weather."

That was the first I heard my mother say that. I felt a twinge of concern, but forgot about it as I got my gear together.

I kept my fanny pack on. It held the basic things that I'd always need, like my whistle, Kleenex, gum, sunscreen, lip balm, Swiss Army knife, water, snack, extra socks, windbreaker and cell phone and sometimes my walkie-talkie. I also kept a variety of other things in there, like my little bird identification book and wrappers from granola bars and gum that I forgot to remove. You know how it is with purses. I need to clean it out and never find the time.

We got in the helicopter and I sat by a window. Happy and John crouched between me and Mom, both in their harnesses and tied securely to a bar on the floor. Normally, tracking dogs ride in crates when we fly in a plane, but in the helicopter we didn't have room.

Riding in a helicopter is a lot different from a plane. There are many ups and downs and quick movements. I kept thinking

I'd fall out even though I wore a lap and shoulder harness. I took deep breaths and looked out the window. Someone once told me that looking outside the vehicle keeps you from getting car sick because your eyes focus on faraway objects. Without my Dramamine I figured I better keep my eyes on the scenery.

As I watched the ground fall away I twirled the spider stud earring in my left ear and thought about Shawn and if he'd be mad at me. I also thought about my *kapucha* team and if they'd think I was doing something important. Probably not. All I could do now was what my Dad told me: the best I can and everything will turn out right.

The short, bald pilot showed us a big grin and white teeth. He put on his headphones then started the engine. I watched as the blades turned slowly, then they moved faster and faster until one blade blended in with the next one and it looked like a solid circle.

"You travel light," the pilot shouted.

"Pretty light," Mom answered. "We have to. I gotta carry all that on my back." Mom smiled back. There was much more to her answer, but since the helicopter was starting she didn't want to yell over the engines.

The helicopter flew nice and straight and I didn't feel too sick. We approached the Oklahoma City airport, that is, the Will Rogers International Airport and the pilot landed next to a military plane.

The big, fat plane was painted dull green with an American flag on the tail. We waited until the blades stopped. "You can get out now," the pilot said. "Here, I'll get those bags for you."

Happy got out and shook like she does after a bath. John jumped out and promptly wet on the pavement.

"Poor thing," Mom said as she stroked John's head. "Doesn't like flying, but she's the best tracker around."

"Ready for your next leg?" The helicopter pilot asked.

"As we'll ever be," Mom answered. A jet streaked down the runway and I covered my ears.

Two airport guys came over with a security guard. The taller of the two men asked for our identification. Mom got out her wallet as did Rowdy. All I have is a library card and I knew he didn't care about that.

"How y'all doin'?" the other man with a short black beard and thick glasses asked.

"Looks like we got some work to do in Arizona," Mom answered.

"This your daughter?" asked the tall guy who looked a lot like my school principal.

"The one and only. She doesn't have a driver's license yet."

He looked from Mom's face to mine. There's clearly enough resemblance to take her word for it. Same dark eyes and black eyebrows and the same straight nose. Our eyebrows are arched which gives us what my Grandma Jaunty calls "that sassy look." My feet are pretty big so I figure that I'll grow up more height-wise and maybe be as tall as Mom.

"Okay," the guy said. "We have to take your gear and run it through the x-ray luggage machine. Won't take but a minute."

"We have knives in those fanny packs," Mom said.

"We know. But we have to check." He loaded our packs onto a carrier and took off towards the terminal.

"They're gonna find all kinds of metal in there," I said.

"They know what's what," Rowdy said. "As long as there isn't a bomb in your bag we'll be okay." He had a wad of gum in his mouth and blew a big bubble.

"You take your Dramamine, honey?" Mom asked. "You look pale."

I shook my head. "I thought I had some in my pack, but they're all gone."

Mom let out a big sigh to tell me she was not happy. She pulled out a tube from her breast pocket where she keeps her vitamins. She fished out a Dramamine tablet. "Here, this isn't the chewable kind."

I swallowed it, grateful that I wouldn't have to fight an upset stomach all the way to Arizona. By that time the guards had returned and dropped our packs by the helicopter.

"We need to check you with the wands," the bearded guy said.

He ran the wands over our bodies to make sure we weren't toting dynamite or something else really dangerous around our waists that might explode, then he gave us a smile.

"Have a nice trip and good luck," the bearded guy said.

Obviously, this is not regular airline procedure where we show tickets and walk through x-ray screens. Even though we didn't have passports officials knew we were coming because the local police called ahead. If all the trackers had been with us we'd have to go through the terminal, fill out forms and the dogs would sit in crates. Luckily again for Happy, John, Barney and Cosmo, they didn't have to ride in crates and got to sit next to us.

Mom has been at this airport several times already and she causes a stir whenever she shows up with the dogs. I noticed that a bunch of people pointed and looked at us through the big window in the terminal.

We climbed into the plane and sat behind the two pilots. They nodded and one asked, "You ready?"

"Anytime," Mom answered as she buckled in.

After takeoff we ate peanut butter and jelly sandwiches and gave the dogs a few hard doggie biscuits. Rowdy's dogs lay down and looked asleep, but they both kept their eyes half open. Happy slept while John whined quietly with her head in my lap.

Almost three hours later we landed at the Flagstaff Pulliam Airport. It's not a big airport and normally only small planes land here. When we got out I felt grateful to be wearing winter clothes. It felt like a cold, gloomy day. The gray sky appeared ready to drop snow. Cold wind hit my neck and snaked down my collar and my back. This definitely looked and felt like lip balm weather.

The German Shepherds put their noses in the air and took deep breaths. The cold, damp breeze and pine trees smelled good to them. Short-haired John would need her jacket tonight.

We followed an airport lady through the terminal. Mom and I went to the ladies room while Rowdy held the dogs. By the time we returned, travelers had gathered around Rowdy and asked the usual questions. Dogs attract a lot of attention and Rowdy would have signed autographs if anyone had asked him.

We let the dogs pee outside in the street in front of the airport. Happy did a poop that Mom gathered in one of the plastic bags she carried specifically for that purpose and dropped it in the garbage.

"So why do you use these dogs?" Asked a large lady in a big red parka, brown jeans and knee-high fuzzy turquoise boots. She wore pink lipstick and a green knitted cap that covered dyed black hair. Rhinestone earrings dangled from her ears. Halloween was a month ago so I had no idea what she might be dressed for.

"Well," I answered in my rehearsed mini-speech that I use when I talk to little kids, "many search and rescue dogs are German Shepherd dogs, mainly because they don't try and find birds and other wildlife when they're out tracking lost people. Plus, their coats protect them from thorns and other scratchy plants. They're smart and strong and they mind well."

"And what about that one with no hair?"

"She's got hair, just not as much. German Shorthair Pointers also are strong and smart, but they like to chase after small things that fly or run. Like birds, squirrels and prairie dogs. Their coats aren't thick enough to protect them in dense thickets. After all, that's why they're called Shorthairs. But they're great searching dogs."

"She looks more like a hunting dog," the lady said. Her pink lipstick had smeared all over her front teeth. She took off a mitten and as she petted John's head, my dog leaned against her. Two of the lady's fingers were weighed down with what looked like giant diamond rings.

"They're actually good searching, hunting and racing dogs," I said. "Mushers who race sled dogs in the United States and in Europe like German Shorthairs because they're determined to run. But winters can be tough on Shorthairs if they don't wear a doggie jacket. Sometimes males wear a special coat to make sure their pee pees don't freeze. In Alaska mushers breed Shorthairs with Alaskan Huskies to create mixed-breeds with more hair."

"Oh, my. How interesting. And where are you going now?"

"Well, there are some lost hunters on the North Rim of the Grand Canyon and . . ."

"Virginia Black Wolf?" a deep voice asked from behind us.

"That's me," Mom answered.

A tall, thin man wearing a cowboy hat, button-down flannel shirt and jeans stuck out his hand. "I'm Orvis Whipple. I'm taking you to the North Rim." He leaned his head to the side and spit out a brown stream of chaw juice.

"How far is it?" Rowdy asked.

"If we were driving, maybe three, four hours. But we're taking the chopper. Ready?"

Mom looked at me and winked. "Lead the way," she said.

The lady with the wild clothes had been listening. "Good luck, deary. What did you say your name was?"

"Tuli Black Wolf. From McAlester, Oklahoma," I answered as Mom yanked my arm and pulled me along with her.

"I'm Sheena Livingston," she yelled to me.

Sheena? That sounded like a jungle name. Anyway, we followed the same traveling routine, only this time with more intriguing scenery. We flew over the San Francisco Peaks, a stunning volcanic range covered with pines and a few patches of aspen trees with white bark. On the west side of the mountain were slashes through the forest, like claw marks across skin.

"Look down there," Orvis yelled. Then he spit into an empty Pepsi can. "That's the Snow Bowl ski resort. See the ski runs that cut through the forest? A month or so ago the oak and aspen leaves were changing. Really pretty red and yellow."

We then flew across what looked to me like desert landscape. Red dirt and scrubby trees dotted the ground. The trees were taller and denser as we got closer to the Canyon. Finally we arrived at the South Rim. I looked down at the sea of vehicles parked at what I thought might be the visitors' center.

"Not as busy as in summer," Orvis said. "Still, too many darn people. The North Rim's a lot different from the South Rim. It's less crowded, is filled with animals and until the Rim closes for the snowy months, camping is quiet and peaceful. You'll probably see deer, condors and other birds.

"In recent years though, rain's been scarce. In some areas rain hasn't fallen for months and the big Ponderosa trees look green and happy, but they're really dry and are being eaten from the inside by the pine beetle. They suck the life right out the trees in a matter of days. There're thousands of brown, dead ponderosas in and around Flagstaff. Those little bugs have done a lot of damage."

"Do you ever see animals?" I asked him.

"Oh, yeah. Deer, antelope, turkeys. There aren't any elk up here on the North Rim. Just deer. Lots of elk in Flagstaff, though. Used to be lots of antelope but now the coyotes are killing them off. In Flagstaff to the south of the Grand Canyon, cougars and bears are moving more and more into the neighborhoods.

Sometimes mountain lions take cats and dogs right off porches. Cougars and bears have to eat, but in the mountains the water's getting scarce. And the animals they usually count on for breakfast, like rabbits, antelope, deer and elk also move around more in order to find water. The predators follow them into backyards and golf courses."

Orvis took us over the canyon. I saw the Colorado River snaking across the bottom. The ribbon of water was a mile down from the Canyon rim and looked it. The North Rim loomed in the distance, tall trees lining the edge like dark green frosting on a cake. We approached rapidly then flew over tree tops for a while then arrived at a clearing where Orvis set us down.

"Only 26 miles between the south and north rim," Orvis said. "Some people do rim-to-rim runs in one day."

"You mean on foot?" I asked. That sounded crazy, to say the least. My knees and ankles hurt just thinking about it.

"Yeah. A few crazy mountain runners used to do rim-to-rim-to-rim, but that's too dangerous and the park won't allow that anymore."

"Sounds tough," said Rowdy.

"It is," Orvis answered. "Twenty three miles or so between rims because of the switchback trails. But it's only eleven miles as the crow flies. Okay, here we are. This is Jacob Lake Inn. No landing pad so we're using the parking lot. You can go inside and use the bathrooms if you want. There's some grocery items in there store if you need something. The cookies are always good."

We hopped out when the blades stopped turning. A group of motorcyclists dressed in heavy riding boots, black leather pants and jackets with bandanas on their heads leaned against the railings in front of the restaurant as they watched us. A few had HELL'S ANGELS painted on the backs of their jackets.

The wind felt cold and brisk and I wondered how they kept their faces from chapping. I put a small amount of glycerin or

Vaseline on my face when I run in windy weather, otherwise my skin begins to flake a few days later.

"Sorry about that," Rowdy said after all the dogs peed then pooped on the lot. "I'll pick it up."

"Okay, I'll let you," Orvis said after he spit. This time he put his finger inside his cheek and pushed out the tobacco. "Your van's over there." He pointed to a green van with tall luggage racks on top and sticking out the back. "That's a firefighting van used by hot shots."

A little blond-haired girl with her hair tucked into an Arizona Diamondbacks cap hopped out of the van and walked over to us. She wore Hot Shot gear and appeared ready to fight a fire.

"I'm Lucy," she said with a big smile. "I'll be driving you to Operations."

We all introduced ourselves then Lucy gave each dog a head scratch. "Oh, I just love dogs," she gushed. "You can put your gear in the back seats. There's enough room for the dogs on the floor."

Rowdy dumped his poop bags in the garbage then we piled into the van and began the last leg of our journey, an almost eight mile ride over the dreaded bumpy dirt roads to the base camp where Mom and Rowdy would begin their search. Lucy talked as she drove, chatting about the snow that was moving towards us, the recent plane crash at the South Rim and a fire that recently had scorched thousands of acres on the North Rim.

"That fire was caused by lightning, but a lot are caused by humans. People just don't know how to put out campfires," she said.

"Oh, they know," Mom countered. "They just don't do it." She's not very forgiving when it comes to careless camping.

"And you may see the condors," Lucy added. "They were released last spring and are doing well. They've been flying around Jacob Lake Inn."

"I've never seen one in the wild," I said. "Only in zoos."

"These condors are great," Lucy said enthusiastically. "Their wings span at least ten feet. You can't miss them. Although some people mistake them for turkeys."

"Turkeys?" Rowdy asked to make sure he heard right. "How do you mistake a condor for a turkey?"

"Same way some hunters mistake a human jogger with a blond pony tail for a white-tailed deer, I guess," was Mom's interesting, yet truthful answer. A woman had been shot in the arm by a deer hunter last year outside of McAlester. The hunter claimed that he thought her bouncing hair was the hind end of a white tailed deer running through the brush.

We drove a few more moments in silence. I looked out the window and rubbed John's neck as she dozed, her head still in my lap. "You could get lost out here," I said.

Mom turned around from where she sat in front of me. "What did you say, honey?"

"Lots of trees. Big forest. You could get lost easily."

Mom laughed and turned back around, her arm draped across the seat back. "Yes, honey. You sure can. That's the situation we have here."

What was my class thinking about me? Mom had told the school I was searching with her. We were now two hours behind Oklahoma time, which meant my friends were eating lunch about now. Were they talking about me? Did they ponder the dangers I might face? Considering that I rarely gave a thought to those who were absent, they probably were talking about the game on Friday.

Lucy held up a folded map. "Here's the map. I circled where you landed and where the Operations camp is."

Mom unfolded the map as Lucy talked. "We're headed out west along 461 then we'll hook up with 462. Then we go south about five miles or so down 22. That's south."

While we made our way down the road I looked out the window while Mom and Rowdy studied the map. Mom has a knack for memorizing landmarks.

"Lots of springs on here," Mom commented.

"Yeah. And a lot of tanks. Not all have water, though," Lucy said.

"Lots of canyons, too."

"Yup. Hundreds of drop-offs. Some are just a few feet while others are dozens or hundreds of feet deep. Of course, you won't mistake the Grand Canyon for a little valley."

We passed three riders on ATVs. Lucy waved as we went past. "What are all these ATVs doing out here?" Rowdy asked. "This sure disrupts the peace and quiet."

"Those are searchers," Lucy said. "They're all over the place today."

Mom and Rowdy looked at each other. Mom shook her head. "Oh, man," Rowdy said quietly.

Lucy veered off the man road into the woods. "Where are you headed?" Mom asked. "Big Springs?"

"No, we go past that. The Operations camp is next to the lost hunters' camp. We turn left on 447, then right on 252. They pitched tents off the road."

We parked to the south of a large camp site. Smoke from at least two fires curled up to the sky between tents, trucks and trailers of various colors. One red tent had an American flag flying proudly from a thirty foot pole sunk into the ground by the entrance. Fifty or so people milled around, many of whom were dressed in camouflage and standing next to their ATVs or horses.

Small groves of oak trees stood under the tall pine trees. Their dried, crunchy red and yellow leaves had fallen off a month ago in October and lay in drifts around the heavy, gnarled trunks. Any other time this would be a wonderful place to camp or hike.

Now it looked like a messy, disorganized camping party with way too many people.

"Is this a revival" I asked.

Mom gave me one of her sighs. "No, but unfortunately it may seem like it."

"Shoot," Rowdy said as he placed two hunks of Double Bubble in his mouth. "There must be a million tracks out there by now."

Mom agreed. "True enough."

"What the problem?" The lady driver asked.

"The problem with lost people," Mom explained, "is that as soon as well-meaning folks find out about them the helpers decide to show up whether they know how to search or not. They want to help and in the process they make matters worse by tromping through the forest and they're completely disorganized."

"But more searchers means there's a better chance of finding the lost people, right?"

"No, not really. All these people wandering around leave their tracks. They cover the tracks of the lost ones. Searchers also fill the air with their cells and that confuses the dogs."

Lucy looked at Mom in the rear view mirror. She didn't understand that and Mom caught her confused look.

"We're all made of cells, right?" Mom started.

The girl nodded.

"Okay. All those dead cells on your skin have bacteria attached to them. That bacteria leaves secretions which gives off the odor of human scent."

"Oh," the girl said. "Like foot odor."

"Yeah, something like that. Dogs search out the lost person by tracking his or her scent. In other words, in the course of helping, all these other people screw things up. They leave tracks and odors besides that of the lost person that confuses trackers and dogs."

"Wow. I didn't know that about body odor and dogs. Cool," Lucy exclaimed.

"Yes, indeedy."

Lucy turned off the engine and Rowdy opened the door. A blast of cold air rushed in. "Man, it's cold," I said. The air smelled damp.

"And I told you it would be, Missy," Mom said. She took her gloves from her fanny pack and put them on. "Where's your hat?"

"Right here. I got it." I had it folded in my jacket pocket.

"Put it on. You need to keep your heat in. It's getting colder as the day grows on."

"It rained last night," Lucy said. "With that front coming through it'll be real cold again tonight."

We led the dogs to the Operations table. The ground litter of oak leaves and pine needles felt soggy, not crunchy like they looked. Because of the rain tracks might be erased in some places. I knew that Mom was measuring what that meant: a very tough search ahead of her.

Maps and radios lay on the large fold-out table. A variety of people stood around drinking coffee and pointing at the maps. White styrofoam cups littered the ground. I've learned that if there is no obvious garbage can available, then people find that an excuse to drop their junk.

An overweight woman who surely couldn't run three miles wearing boots and a loaded pack stood next to her Golden Retriever, a dog that looked pretty darn fit. Another tough, lean man who looked like a Marine held a puppy that was years away from assisting in any search. A teenaged boy tried to pet his agitated German Shepherd who acted like she might bite.

Another woman was obviously a runner and ready for action, but she had no dog.

"You the Oklahoma Unit?" asked a gray haired man dressed in hunting gear. He wore a pistol in a holster around his waist and he looked more like an actor in a combat movie than a search and rescue worker.

"Yes, I'm Virginia Black Wolf," Mom said in her commanding voice. The others turned and looked her up and down. Mom looks pretty cool in her shades and search outfit.

"I'm the Operational Leader, Mickey Taylor," the man said. He shook Mom's hand.

Mom looked to Rowdy and me then introduced us. "This is Rowdy Willard and my daughter Tuli."

"Well, I'm glad to finally meet you Virginia. That article in People about you was pretty darn interesting. My son wants to meet you."

"He in school?" Mom asked. She assumed he was in grade school like the Boy Scouts she teaches.

"Nope. He's a Navy SEAL."

"Hmmm." She wasn't too surprised. She gets all kinds of people asking her advice, even the military.

Several of the people around the table looked at Mom and whispered. They do that at the grocery store and the mall. Mom's pretty distinctive looking and has a face you don't forget. I hope I look like her someday. Every now and then someone asks for an autograph. They get nervous and hand her an orange or something else silly to sign.

Mickey continued. "The Forest Service already has some men and women out looking. As you can maybe tell, the newly formed Northern Arizona Search and Rescue Unit is trying to help. We have a couple of folks from Utah who are training with us. We just aren't quite ready yet."

Mom glanced at the novice trackers. "Gotta start someplace," she said. "But I suggest you not send anyone out to search if they don't know how to get back. You'll create more problems than you already have. Now, get me up to date."

Mickey then told Mom pretty much the same thing the Sheriff already told her. "Four males, that's three adults and one juvenile, didn't check in last night. A Jody Johnston and his son. His name's Jody, too."

"I heard that already."

"Yeah, well. Then there's Frank Martin and Stan Wallace. Their wives are friends and they called each other to compare notes. None of them heard from their husbands. One lady called the Flagstaff Sheriff around two this morning. Just so you know, Frank Martin had his knee replaced only six months ago."

"And he thought he'd kill a deer and drag it for miles back to his truck?" Rowdy asked. That's a good question. No one in our family hunts, but I get to hear a lot about it. Sometimes a hunter kills a deer far from his vehicle and has to bring it back somehow. Taking out the guts helps some, although the deer can still be heavy to drag when the hunter is tired. Having a new knee would make dragging pretty much impossible.

"Maybe he planned on doing a drive-by shooting," Mickey answered. "Some hunters do that, you know. It's kind of like trolling for fish. They drive around and shoot from the vehicle."

"That's real fair," Mom said in her I-hate-hunting voice.

"Well, it's the reality of the sport. But these guys didn't do that yesterday. They walked." Mickey paused to sip his coffee. "So, you got at least one gimpy guy out there. I don't know about the health of the others."

"What have you found so far?" Mom asked.

"Nothing. Three Forest Service women on horses were out all day. Every time they came back with no word about tracks. They found some locked camping trailers close by, but hunters often leave them when they plan to hunt several weekends. It's a lot easier to leave the trailers here between hunts than to drag them off the hill and then back again. No tracks around any of them. Course, it rained last night and there probably aren't any left to find."

"Hard for the dogs to scent, too," Rowdy said. "Rain can really wipe out prints."

"Maybe," Mom said as she tapped Happy's head with her forefinger. "Maybe not." She knows that foot prints aren't the only tracks people leave behind.

"How many trackers are out now?" Rowdy asked.

"No trackers. At least no professional trackers. The Forest Service people know more about this kind of thing than anyone else here. I have no idea how many other people are hiking around." He put his hands on his hips and took a deep breath of cold air. "I've been trying to keep this search under control and every time I turn around another group takes off on its own."

"Not good," Mom said. "But that's what happens when you let too many people know a search has started. Anyone know what the lost men are carrying?"

"The wives say they had all kinds of clothes and equipment. They went shopping before they came to the Rim and one complained about how much her husband spent on the Cabela Outfitter's web site."

"Do they have coats?" Mom zipped her jacket and adjusted the collar.

Mickey shrugged. "Not sure. Hope so. I can't see how they'd survive without a coat."

"What about a GPS?" That's a Global Positioning System that works by using satellites. The signal a GPS receives comes from the satellite and tells the user where he or she is on the ground. Mom says that the GPS measures distance using the travel time of radio signals. The GPS I'm learning to use hangs around my neck and is the size of a large cell phone. Once I figure it out then I'll be able to tell where I am in a forest. Mom isn't too keen on using one because if the satellites fail we'll have to use a map and compass. She says we may as well depend on the old fashioned way of getting around.

"Where is the PLS?" That stands for the Point Last Seen. It could be that someone saw the missing men in their camp site. It might be that someone saw them on a trail or road before they became lost. Mom put on some lip balm and started to clean her glasses. I knew that as soon as she had enough information she'd take off into the woods.

"We know they left from their camp site," Mickey said. "It's over there. We know they were here because they told a gas station guy at Jacob Lake they were coming to 252. Evidently, a friend told them it was a good place to set up camp. It didn't take long for the Forest Service to find it, although nobody actually saw them in their camp. The next closest campsite that we know of is about a quarter mile west of here and the hunters camped there didn't see anyone else. It's a big forest."

Mickey pointed to a grove of trees about 100 feet to the south of the table. "That's their site." I saw two trucks, three tents, a bunch of camping gear strewn around, and at least twenty people wandering through the lost hunters' camp.

"Oh swell," Mom said.

It was a problem. With so many people mingling around the tracks would be ruined and their smells would cover up the odors of the men we needed to find.

Mickey shrugged. "Never underestimate the desire of the home crowd to get involved. I tried, but there're no plans, no master map, and everyone's tuned to the frequency of the one radio we got at the table. It's a free-for-all." Mickey paused for a few seconds. "Hey, my grandma's a full blood Cherokee," he said.

"That's nice," Mom answered without interest. A lot of people say that and she basically ignores them. Even if they don't know for sure if they are Indian they like to say they are. And they always seem to pick Cherokee as their tribe. I mean, what are we supposed to say when someone says they're part Indian? It's interesting that real Indians never say that.

"Rowdy," Mom said. "Let's get over to their camp."

"Getting' late," Rowdy said.

"Yes it is," Mom agreed. "But we can do a quick search before dark."

Our small group of four humans and four dogs walked to the hunter's camp. Any tracks that may have been left by the four hunters were completely covered, courtesy of the crowd of searchers who by this time were aimlessly wandering through the woods. They no doubt hoped the lost guys were sitting around a nearby campfire roasting marshmallows.

"We need scent articles," Mom said to Rowdy.

"Let's see what we can find," he said.

Luckily for us, two of the men had a bag of dirty clothes. A stiff and smelly camouflage shirt stuck out of one laundry sack that sat atop one sleeping bag and a t-shirt with arm pit stains hung out of another. The kid left amazingly stinky socks on top of his bag. The fourth person left no used clothing behind so Mom took his pillow case off his pillow.

Mom handed Rowdy the shirts and pillow case while she gingerly picked up the socks and some scary looking used underwear. Then she led Rowdy and the dogs away from the camp into the trees so the others wouldn't see what we were up to.

Mom laid the clothes on the ground so the dogs could go from one smelly item to the other. Actually, this was sensory overload, but if they got a good whiff of one person maybe they'd find that stinky hunter and the others would be with him.

"I'd bet real money the dogs are going to recall the scent of those socks forever," Mom said.

"I sure hope I don't," I said.

All four dogs put their noses in the air, then to the ground, then to the air again and pulled at the leashes in the same direction. "Ready?" Mom asked Rowdy.

"Yep."

Mom turned to me. "Tuli, you know what to do. Get the tent up and start camp. Don't go anywhere."

"I won't."

"I mean it."

At that moment, I wondered why she felt like she had to make a big deal about me staying in camp. Mom tells me that all women have intuition, but not all of them listen to it. Mom listens to hers very carefully which made me question myself. Did I had a subconscious thought that Mom recognized and I didn't?

Mom released Happy and John at the same time. The dogs took off to the southwest through the trees. Then Rowdy unleashed Barney and Cosmo. Mom and Rowdy followed them easily since the dogs zig zagged back and forth trying to zoom in on a scent. If viewed from above, their movements would look like they were moving left to right to left again, each length shorter than the one before, as if ping-ponging back and forth within a triangle or cone.

Hopefully, at the tip of the triangle would be what they were looking for: the lost hunters. All four dogs moved in the same general direction, although they stayed about fifty feet apart from each other.

Mom and Rowdy disappeared into the forest. I turned back to camp, knowing that I needed to find a dry, secure spot. Mom, Rowdy and the dogs would need a comfortable place to rest. I had to make certain the tents and dinner were prepared. It's not fun to work a hard search then to return to camp with no place warm to sleep and nothing to eat and drink.

I wandered back to the Operations table and asked Mickey where we could camp.

"Any old place you want. I'd stay away from that road since there's no telling who else is going to come through here. Some of these people are driving way too fast."

I started to walk to the edge of the clearing, then thought of something. "Hey, Mickey," I asked him. He looked up from his map. "Are there mountain lions here?"

"Oh, heck yes. Why?"

"Uh, just wondering." I hesitated to tell him my concerns. Five years ago we had gone to Glacier National Park and I was surprised, happy and very scared, actually, to see so many wild animals everywhere. I mean, we saw grizzlies and black bears eating berries by the side of the road. Big-horned sheep and mountain goats stood next to the hiking trails above the Logan Pass ranger station.

What scared me the most was what the ranger told me while our family ate lunch in our car next to the forest at Two Medicine: "You all be real careful. Bears have been known to come right out of the woods by the parking lot and take people's food. One did last week. Right where you're parked. Have a nice day!"

Since then I always had it in my head that lions, bears and Jaws the Shark could jump from the woods and water and drag me away.

"Don't worry," Mickey said as he looked at my expression. "Lions wouldn't come near this place. Would you?"

We looked around at the tents, ATVs and trucks, dozens of campfires and people milling around. Now that I thought about it, there were no outhouses. Yes, things could get pretty stinky before too long.

I laughed. "I guess not."

"You'll see coyotes, foxes, squirrels, mule deer, coyotes, and probably turkeys. It's a nice place, usually."

So I picked a nice spot away from the crowd under tall pines with low limbs. I got our camping bags and lay two tarps on the pine-covered ground. I kept one eye on the edge of the tress as I set up a tent for me and Mom and another for Rowdy.

We didn't have many bags. Trackers often carry enough food and water for themselves and their animals for three or four days, but they normally don't stay out that long. Their day packs aren't large like packs you might take on an extended camping trip into the Grand Canyon.

Most trackers return to base camp several times a day to regroup and to receive updates and instructions. Some searchers who use horses in the mountains can't afford to backtrack to camp repeatedly, so they stay out longer and they carry more and bigger packs.

Trackers are prepared to stay out in the environment if they have to, but most lost people never expect to get lost. Which is why they often die. They don't have the proper clothes or gear to help them survive. That includes hunters, hikers and Boy Scouts who should know better. After years of searching in a variety of environments, Mom knows exactly what she needs for every kind of weather and she travels with a bare minimum of equipment. Every ounce counts. Even the handle of her toothbrush is cut off close to the head.

I thought about the men that Mom and Rowdy searched for as I pulled the heavy wire of the gang line between two trees for the four dogs. I wrapped one end of the line around one trunk and attached the end to the line with a metal clip. Then I did the same with the other end of the line on the other trunk. Separate lines hung downwards three feet apart and were attached to the main line. The dogs were clipped to those lines, like on leashes. If it wasn't too cold they'd stay out tonight. But if it rained or snowed they'd come into the tents with us.

I nibbled on a granola bar as I walked around the camp looking for familiar faces. I didn't see any. Many of the trackers I had met on other searches with Mom were now someplace else and I wasn't surprised to see that more inexperienced searchers had arrived. They were mainly good ol' boys with guns and pick up trucks. They meant well, but didn't know the ins and outs of a search.

Another dog from the Northern Arizona unit wouldn't start. The Golden Retriever and her owner stood at the edge of the forest where Mom and Rowdy had begun their search. The female owner kept urging the Golden Retriever to follow Mom and Rowdy, but the Retriever sat looking at her master, whimpering like an insecure puppy. The handler tugged at the leash a few times trying to get it motivated. The dog stood, then sat.

I looked at the handler's vehicle, a beat up old Dodge truck with an exhaust pipe hanging by a coat hanger. "You always drive that truck?" I asked her.

She gave me a look that meant she was insulted. "No, I don't. Why do you want to know?"

I knelt down and scratched the dog's head. She licked my face and whined. "How often does your dog refuse to start?"

"Not a lot. Last time was about a month ago. I don't know what do to. She looked at me closer. Hey, is your mom Virginia Black Wolf?"

"That's her."

"So, you might know what's wrong with my dog?"

"Maybe. What did you drive a month ago?"

"This truck."

"You may want to drive another car when you have to work with your dog. A truck this old probably has a poor emission system. Hydrogen sulfide paralyzes his olfactory function."

Yes, I'm quite the walking encyclopedia, aren't I? What I told that lady was that the truck spews out black smoke from the tail pipe and the nasty air blocks the dog's ability to smell.

The lady stood with her mouth open looking at me.

"Well, it does," I said. I love being a smart kid. "I learned that last month at a tracking seminar in Dallas."

She thought about what I said for a moment as she looked at the truck's tail pipe, then said, "How long will it take before she can smell?"

"Maybe tomorrow. Maybe today. Hard to tell. Depends on the dog."

Her dog panted and rubbed her head against my hand, wanting more attention. "This is a good dog. Just give her time."

"Thanks," she said to me. "Well, Lady," she said to her dog, "let's have dinner."

I left Lady and her human at the forest edge then went back to my camp to fill water bowls for the dogs. Even though it rained the night before, I found dry kindling under the wet needles and quickly made a nice hot fire. I was busy stirring a pot of beans when Mom and Rowdy returned.

All four dogs went obediently to the gang line, then lay down, panting hard in between laps from the bowls of water I'd put out for each one of them. From the look on Mom's face she was unsuccessful in her search.

Mom took off her pack and tossed the heavy bag into the tent. Since she had probably taken nothing out of it during the day, the pack would be ready to go again tomorrow. She drank red Gatorade from a plastic bottle as she sat in the entryway of the tent.

"Anything?" I asked.

She shook her head. "Got dark and we had to come back. *Kafi is sam atahali tuk o?*-Did you make me coffee?"

"Yes, I made coffee." Mom usually only drinks decaffeinated coffee in the mornings. But on searches she drinks a lot of the caffeinated kind to keep her awake.

"Too many tracks," Rowdy said from the gang line where he took off his dogs' light packs. Unless it's hot, many dogs carry their own saddle bag packs containing their food, water and dog supplies.

"Everywhere," Mom agreed. "But the dogs were eager and wanted to go southwest first, then they turned and went north as far as a big green tank. It had a ladder up the side. There were tracks-four sets of prints-all around it."

"You mean that tank near 252C and 252," Mickey offered.

"Maybe," Mom answered. "Then the tracks went back to the southwest. In a round-about way. They're walking in big circles and are leaving their smell all over the countryside."

She took off her fanny pack and heavy coat and put on a wool sweater and down vest. Even thought she felt warm right now, I knew Mom would get chilled quickly. We're alike in that we get cold easily and do better in warm weather.

"I'm going to Operations for a map. What else you got in that pot besides beans?" she asked in a grumpy tone.

"I cut up some turkey dogs, a can of stewed tomatoes, a can of carrots and there's rolls in the bag."

"Hmmm," was all Mom said. That sound meant volumes.

See, when Dad knows that Mom would be tired after a long day of tracking or training, he'd make her favorite dinner: spinach salad with avocado and lots of cherry tomatoes, steamed asparagus that she dipped into Italian dressing and roasted chicken breasts with the skins off and covered with sautéed mushrooms and steak sauce. Beans and turkey dogs sopped up with white bread rolls aren't exactly her favorites.

"I wish it were more," I said.

Mom took out a diaper wipe and cleaned her face. "It'll do," she said before she stood and walked off to the table. I knew this wasn't her ideal meal. And she knows it's never my fault that we have to eat canned food when we're camping. I like Beenie Weenies, but Mom thinks we should cook from scratch as much as possible at home.

Mom and Rowdy returned from the Operations table with a map of the North Rim. As I spooned the beans into bowls for them, Rowdy held the flashlight as they looked at the map of the North Kaibab Ranger District they had spread on the ground. Normally, Mom would study a map before going out on a search, but it was late when we arrived and she didn't have time.

"We should go back to where we were," Mom said. "The dogs were still eager."

"I agree," said Rowdy.

"Pine Hollow Trick Tank is in that direction. How much of a hollow is it?"

"Beats me. We need to ask Mickey. I have a feeling that there are a lot of drop-offs around here."

"There are a lot of drop offs," Mickey said from behind Mom and Rowdy. He pointed to the map. "See, all these roads, like 255, and 417 south of that. Then the roads 218 and 218B are like fingers with valleys on each side of them. You can branch off in a lot of directions. Smaller roads are everywhere. Good deer country."

"I can see that," Mom said.

"These guys could be in a valley, at the bottom of a steep drop off. Man, it's a big area." Rowdy has a way of stating the obvious.

"Tough to kill a deer and haul it back to your vehicle, "Mom added.

"Sure is," Mickey said. "I've done it. Well, thought you'd want to know the weather service just said rain's coming in the morning."

"We need to start early," Mom said.

"Okay. My tent's the red one if you need anything."

"The one with the big American flag?" I asked.

"No, I'm behind that one. The flag belongs to a Utah group. Night. Sleep tight."

Mickey went back to his table. We ate our beans and rolls. I fed the dogs hard kibble mixed with a few cans of soft food then poured warm water on top so they wouldn't choke. Afterwards, each got a doggy biscuit and a vitamin.

After cleaning the pot and the bowls I found more kindling for a fire the next morning and covered it with a small tarp. Then I checked the dogs and got into the tent. I unrolled the bags and blew up the inflatable pillows. Normally I like three pillows, two under my head and one between my knees when I lay on my side. That keeps my leg and back from aching. One dinky little pillow for my neck is no fun.

Mom and Rowdy went back to the Operations table for a few more hours, taking in all the information they could gather. I heard Mom come into the tent.

"What did you decide?" I asked her as she took off her boots and outer clothes.

"We have to get started early." Mom pulled on another wool sweater and some heavy sweat pants, then re-braided her hair and put on a wool hat. "Those men are in trouble right now and we have to find them in the next day or two. I'm willing to bet they can't manage longer than that."

Mom slipped into her bag, zipped it up and sighed deeply as her head hit the inflatable pillow. "You need to sleep, honey. No telling what may happen tomorrow."

I lay there looking up at the ceiling of the tent. If it were warm, we'd take off the rain fly so the breeze would come in and we could see the stars. But tonight, it was so cold I put on my coat, gloves and hat. Even inside my super-insulated down bag I shivered and wished for summer.

As I listened to the voices in the camp, the truck engines and the clanging of metal utensils, I visualized Shawn and how I'd train even harder when I got home. My mental training schedule came easily. My mental chart told me how far I'd run every day and how I'd get Mom and Dad to practice *kapucha* with me. By the time my winning strategy was all worked out, I was asleep.

Many hours later Mom unzipped her bag. Then she put on her coat and boots and climbed out of the tent. She and Rowdy spoke in low voices as they got the dogs ready. I unzipped my bag in a hurry and put on my boots that sat inside by the door.

I emerged from the tent to see the first hint of daylight through thick clouds. The camp started buzzing with activity. Engines started and horses whinnied. I stomped my feet and noticed that our fire had not been lit. That meant Mom and Rowdy were about to start the day without anything hot to eat or drink.

My lighter was in my coat pocket and as I clicked it furiously trying to get a flame, Mom put her hand on my arm. "Forget it, honey," she said. "We'll grab some coffee at the Operations table. I have a couple of granola bars and Rowdy has jerky. Take your time."

Then she fastened her pack strap and walked away, John and Happy on either side of her.

The air felt cold in my throat and I needed something hot to drink. I also felt anxious to see what the day would bring, but little did I realize just how exciting it would turn out.

Chapter 5: Emergency Madness

To get my mind off Mom and Rowdy I ate an egg and shredded potato burrito provided by some volunteer cooks from Kanab. Since I hate the feeling of being dirty while camping I brushed and flossed, took my vitamin then found Mickey and asked what was going on so far that morning.

"Well, nothing much. Some riders went out after your mother left and . . ."

"Mickey!" Yelled a woman at the Operations table. "Trouble!"

Mickey ran over to the radio and I followed him. He listened as a panicked male voice on the other end spoke loud and fast.

"We need help now! A horse went over the edge with a rider!" Then static.

"Hello!" Mickey yelled, thinking that yelling might cause the static to disappear.

"Julie fell and broke her leg," the voice on the radio screamed. "It's a compound fracture of her, of her . . .thigh. The horse fell too. He's pretty much okay, but he's got a big cut on his rump. We can't get him out of the canyon because he's completely freaked. We need a truck, a trailer and a backboard!"

As I stood there listening to the scared voice, I thought about how the person on the other end had violated rules of the airways during search and rescue operations. Mom was very specific about how to use a radio during a search.

"You're not supposed to blurt out anything regarding deaths and accidents," Mom had told me. "A relative might be standing close by and can overhear the conversation. How would you feel if you heard over the radio that your relative was dead or dying?"

"I wouldn't," I told her.

"Not only that, other people can listen in to radio conversations, just like they can with walkie talkies and sometimes cell phones. Many people listen to police scanners because they like to hear about wreaks, shootings and such, but others listen so they can be among the first on the scene of an interesting bad accident or house fire."

"So what do you say, then?"

"Skilled workers know they're supposed to use codes to communicate serious problems."

Of course, I hadn't learned radio codes yet. But Mom was right. If a lot of people had been standing around the table to hear what was said, there could have been a frenzy of mass hysteria, rumors and excited people running off into the woods. But up here on the North Rim not too many eavesdroppers heard what the voice had told us.

Several men standing behind me did hear the exchange. "I got a backboard in my truck," said a red head with a burr cut. "Get their location."

Mickey got their bearings. I heard him say road 447, and then he continued the discussion with the radio voice while the campers ran around like ants with their hill knocked over.

I knew that a broken femur, that's the thigh bone, would be painful and dangerous. The big bone's jagged edges could easily cut through arteries and muscle. Riding in a truck on a bumpy road would test the injured woman's ability to deal with some real agony. I hoped they'd get a helicopter here.

Almost all the ATVs in the camp were gone already and several people had ridden away on mountain bikes. It's interesting to me that whenever there's an emergency, people want to get in on the action even if they have no idea what to do and aren't even certain where to go. They need to do something to make themselves feel better. At least most of the camp hadn't heard the radio message.

After an hour of complete chaos, the camp grew quiet. Most people had been out and about since dawn. Others assisted with the injured woman and horse, were looking for the lost hunters' trail, or were busily getting lost themselves.

The day grew colder and I shivered even though I wore heavy clothes. I stood by the operations table, focusing on the map that had little colored pins stuck all over it. I found our base camp and could only speculate where Mom and Rowdy went. I saw where Mickey had made a red circle to mark the horse and rider accident.

No one hung around the Operations table except me, so when the radio squawked I jumped. "Base One, Base One," someone yelled into the radio. "Do you read? Do you read?" It was a man's voice. Deep and booming. And gravelly, like he smoked cigarettes and inhaled deeply.

One of the skills that search and rescue people must learn is to operate a radio. I had the basics down, but still didn't know codes. I pressed the button and replied. "Base One. I read you. This is Tuli Black Wolf. Over."

Pete and I have walkie talkies at home and we pretend we're lost. It's good practice for the real thing. Still, I felt nervous and hoped that he didn't have a problem like the last caller.

"Base One, we have an emergency. Over."

My stomach lurched. I grabbed the radio to take with me as I searched the camp for Mickey.

"I copy that," I replied as I searched frantically for Mickey. Where was he anyway? "Tell me what happened. Over."

Where was Mickey? I slowly jogged around camp and only saw a few people here and there, such as the volunteer cooks who probably didn't know about searching.

"An ATV flipped and the rider is knocked out," Mr. Smoker said quickly. "We need assistance. Over."

So. Here I was. The moment of truth. I mean, what was I supposed to do? I tried to swallow and had difficulty finding spit in my mouth. I took a deep breath then said:

"I read you. Is he breathing? Over."

"Yeah, he's breathing. But he's knocked out. Over."

"Well, he's going to be cold, so you need to cover him with another coat. And don't move him. Over."

"Okay. Okay." He stopped saying 'over.' Stress can do that.

What else should I say? I wondered. Maybe if I kept him talking he'd calm down. Maybe I'd calm down.

"Who is this? Over."

"My name's Jimmy Joe."

"Okay, Jimmy Joe. Where are you? What's your position? You got a map? Over." I ran back to the map and looked down, waiting for him to reply.

"I don't know," he finally managed.

Now, as you might imagine, that's not a good answer. Mom told me and Pete many times about the consequences of going out into the woods, getting lost and/or hurt, and not being able to read a map. This is the perfect example of a major problem.

"I read you. Oh, man." He sounded like he was crying. With a name like Jimmy Joe, I'd cry, too.

"Okay, Jimmy Joe. Here's the deal." I took another deep breath and thought about what Mom might say and this is what I came up with: "If you don't know where you are on the map, then you need to tell me how far you went from camp and in what direction. What are some landmarks around you? You say the rider flipped. That means he was going up or downhill. Correct? Over."

Jimmy Joe sniffed loudly then replied. "Yeah. We was goin' up hill and Bobby flipped over backwards. Oh, man. What if he dies?"

That was a good question, but I wasn't going to talk about death and dying right now. "Jimmy Joe," I said in my best, deep adult voice. "Stay with me. Is he still breathing? Over."

"Yeah. His nose and ears are bleeding."

A head injury. This could be worse than the broken femur. "Jimmy Joe. How far did you ride this morning? Which direction from camp? Over."

"Well, uh. We went north. Like everyone else. Then we got word over the radio about the horse. You know. We tried to go that away."

"So that means you turned and went south. Correct? Over."

"Yeah. Yeah we did. 'Cause the sun was to our left."

I looked at the map and thought I had this figured. So you're in a canyon. There're walls around you. Correct? Over."

I saw a shadow cross the table. Mickey held a cup of hot chocolate. He heard my last statement to Jimmy Joe. He looked at me like my hair was on fire.

"Yeah. Sort of. This road goes straight up, but we didn't go on the road. We went to the side of the road." Jimmy Joe was crying full out now and bursts of static came through the radio. I hoped he had a Kleenex. Otherwise, his sleeve sure would be gross about now.

"Jimmy Joe," I looked at Mickey as I spoke. "Listen carefully. You have to keep your friend warm. You have to make sure he doesn't chill. If you don't have any other clothes then lay down next to him. Got it? We're on our way. Over."

"Hurry. Please hurry." More sniffing and crying.

"Mickey, here," I pointed on the map. "I figure he's about here, down 447 where Mom and Rowdy went. His friend flipped an ATV and is unconscious."

"Oh, no. Not again."

"We have to move on this," I said. "I'll keep talking to him while you get some people together."

Mickey looked at the map. "I know where he is. What's he doing off of 447? That's a heck of a steep road and I can't imagine going up hill through the trees and brush."

"Beats me," I answered.

As Mickey took off and rounded up two women and one man to ride out in a Dodge duely pick-up, I talked to Jimmy Joe.

"Jimmy Joe, this is Tuli Black Wolf here. How're you doing? Over."

"Uh, okay. I'm layin' next to Bobby. Oh, man," he moaned. "How could this happen?"

So I said to myself: Well, Jimmy, if you really wanted me to answer, I'd say that you took off too fast and didn't know where you were headed. In your hurry to find the hurt woman you went straight up a steep hill, not the established road. Now your friend is suffering the consequences of not wearing a helmet.

But Jimmy Joe wasn't really asking me, so I didn't tell him.

Jimmy Joe and I went on like this for another half-an-hour. I felt sick to my stomach and wished that Mickey and his group would hurry. Finally, and as I was about to sit on the ground to steady my thinking, Mickey called to let me know they had arrived at the scene of the accident.

"We're here, Tuli," Mickey said. "We have another hot shot van here and a paramedic who came in on motorcycle from Jacob's Lake. We need to get this guy to the hospital. I'll be back in a few hours. Can you man the table? Over."

"Sure. Don't worry. Over."

"You're doing good, kid. Over."

Well, up until this point, I was only doing what I knew I was supposed to do. When Mickey asked me to take over, I felt even sicker. What if this happened again? What if someone else really got hurt? My hands shook and I felt like I do when I'm about to vomit. If my team saw me now and how nervous I was, I'd never get over it.

"Base One, Base One, do you read?" Came a loud voice over the radio. "We need assistance. Over." It was a woman's voice.

I took in a sharp breath. It sure sounded like my mother.

Chapter 6: My Big Decision

"Mom? This is Tuli. Over."

"Tuli? What are you doing on the radio? Where's Mickey? Over."

My feelings were hurt because Mom decided that I shouldn't be on the radio. And, she hadn't even asked why I was manning the station. Since she made me mad, I didn't feel sick anymore. I know that vomiting doesn't impress Mom.

"Mom, everyone's gone. There've been two accidents. A woman fell off her horse and down a cliff. Then another guy fell off his ATV. Lots of people are out helping. Over."

Mom let out a good sized-curse. She knew better than to do that over the radio. "Well, we need help. We ran into some barbed wire. Happy's paws are punctured and John's are cut. Neither can walk. We need a vehicle to get us back. Over."

"Are they bleeding? Over?"

"Tuli. There's no time for that. Get someone on the radio. Hop to it. Over."

"I read you Mom, but I'm manning the radio. I'll see if I can find someone to help. Over."

Mom made me feel like a child right then, but deep inside I knew that I was doing the right thing and that's what kept me from crying. I could cry later in the tent where no one would see me. For now, I had to find help.

I paced over to where a young man with thick brown hair cut straight at his shoulders sat in front of a fire. An ugly orange truck behind sat behind him. It had been jacked up and adorned with giant tires and many fog lights. I know from experience that often times these kinds of trucks are only for show. Hopefully, this guy could do something with his rig.

"Excuse me," I said to the young man who busily cleaned his fingernails. He looked to be a teen-ager, his face spotted with acne that he'd been picking. He had great hair, though. Anyway, I figured he was left behind to do the grunge work for someone. "We have a problem and need someone to get a team out," I told him.

He jumped up. "What's wrong?"

"It's my mom. She and her dogs ran into some barbed wire. The dogs are cut up and someone needs to go get them."

"Heck yes. Let's do it."

We went back to the operations table and I called Mom while we looked at the map. Mom knows how to read a map very fast. She can go from point A to point B with a compass and expects me and Pete to learn how to do the same.

"Mom, I have someone here who can come get you. Tell me your position. Over."

"Go to the juncture of 447 and 255. See it on the map? Over."

"Yes, I see it. Over."

"Look south to where it says 'Sawmill.' We're a bit south of that. These hunters are wandering all over the place. Over."

"Got it," the young man said. Then he sprinted to his truck.

"Mom," I told her. "A guy in an orange truck is on his way. Over."

"And you? Over."

"Mom, I gotta stay here. One thing after the other is happening and there's no one else here except some volunteer cooks. Over."

She didn't say anything for a few seconds. "See if you can find a vet. Over and out."

After making sure the interior of the tent was neat and asking the cooks if they'd prepare a lunch for Mom and Rowdy, I asked around for a doctor. Then I sat at the Operations table and waited.

Less than an hour later the orange truck drove up with Mom, Rowdy and the dogs in the back. Mom directed the kid to stop at our tent. She jumped out, opened the tailgate and gently lifted the dogs out, one by one. Happy weighs almost 80 pounds and Mom's face turned red with the effort.

Mom had wrapped John's front feet with gauze and tape, but the blood leaked through. John looked like she had stepped in red paint. Happy's feet didn't look any better, wrapped up and soaked through with blood.

I took off the dogs' packs and lifted John's right foot to look at it.

"Put it down, Tuli," Mom said. "Don't touch. It was hard to get that blood to stop. Did you find a vet?"

"No, I didn't. There isn't a vet in camp right now. The only doctor I know of went out to see about that woman who fell this morning. There wasn't even a doctor to look at the guy who fell off his ATV, but a paramedic fireman came from another direction in a hot shot truck."

Rowdy limped over from the truck.

"What's wrong with you?" I asked.

"Knee hurts. I played touch football last weekend and twisted it again."

"There's an ice chest over by that big blue and white tent," I said. "You should ice it."

"Yeah, maybe for a few minutes. I'm cold already."

"Your lips are blue. Maybe you should go to the big tent and sit by the heater."

"Yeah. I should." Then he limped to the operations table for some hot coffee.

Swell, I thought to myself. Now Rowdy's out. He did this same thing a year ago when the team had to find a woman who wandered off from a nursing home. I had wondered then if his knee was really hurt, or if just acted like it did when he got tired. I doubted I'd ever get an answer about that.

"What happened, Mom?"

She looked in a bad mood. John must have really cut herself badly. I looked at the dogs. Happy and John lay on their sides, panting and wide-eyed. John rarely lies still unless she's sleeping. I put my hand on her head and she calmed a little.

"The dogs found scent again almost immediately," she used a baby wipe to clean blood off her hands. "We were tired by the time we got to the spot where we stopped last night. Should have taken a horse or an ATV out there." Her left eye was red and tearing badly. She took out a small mirror from her fanny pack and looked in her eye. She used the edge of a Kleenex to gently push out an eyelash. "That's been bugging me for an hour."

"Dogs are calm," I observed.

"They know to be still. After a few minutes rest I told the dogs to start again and we looked another two hours. I wasn't surprised that hunters were drifting around like balloons. They went to Pine Hollow Trick Tank then south and east back up a hill. I doubt if they have a compass."

Mom took a drink from her Gatorade bottle. "I looked at the topographic map and figured we were only a mile or two from camp, although with their wandering they've covered at least five, maybe eight miles. Then Happy hit barbed wire. When John ran over to see what she was screaming about, she got tangled in it. She's lucky the barbs didn't cut her eyes."

I looked at Rowdy who was now drinking hot coffee and icing his knee by the fire. It was a funny sight, considering the cold weather. I was proud to see that he hadn't gone into the big tent yet.

"It wasn't easy keeping Rowdy's dogs away," Mom said. "Cosmo growled at me."

Cosmo and Barney lay quietly under the gang line, their heads on their paws. "They look pretty scared."

"They may be scared, Tuli, but growling isn't an option in this business." I knew that meant Cosmo was out as a tracker dog. What if he was searching for a child and then once he found it, then growled? When a dog finds a lost person they're supposed to be a welcome sight, not to scare them and certainly not to bite. I doubted that Cosmo would bite anyone, but Mom would never take that chance. She would deal with Rowdy and the dog when we got home.

Mom took out a map she carried folded in her breast pocket. "Here's where we stopped last night." She pointed to a spot half way down 252C. I noticed that her fingernails had much dried blood under them.

"And this is where we went today, down 447 then we went south off the road. The barbed wire is here, next to an old post. I should have noticed it." She threw down her baby wipe in disgust.

This was typical of Mom. She thought she could have changed the course of events "if only she had known." The dogs always run out ahead of her. How could she have known about the barbed wire?

Three trucks roared back into camp, one of them driven by Mickey. Mom got up and scurried over to him. I followed.

"I need a vet," she told him. "And you need to get rid of at least half the people out messing up the ground."

"That's gonna be hard," Mickey replied. He had on a black cap with the Marines logo on it.

"Doesn't matter. You've got people hurt and it can only get worse if rains and they get chilled."

"Maybe we should," said a tall man behind Mickey. "No use in risking people and plowing over familiar ground every day."

"Is there a doctor here or not?" Mom asked again.

"I'm a doctor," the tall man answered. "Reno Perkins," he held out his hand. Mom gave it a quick, hard shake. "My gear's in that green Toyota truck over there." He looked tired and probably wasn't in a mood to get in an argument with my mother.

Mom followed Dr. Perkins to his truck. They exchanged words as he got out his bag of doctor stuff then he followed her to where our dogs waited. I wasn't going to miss this for anything.

Rowdy and I watched Dr. Perkins give John an injection of something that made her eyes droop. A bunch of ATV riders also returned to camp and gathered around to watch the doctor work on John's feet. Our dog was obviously very sleepy but awake. She looked around at all the people and wagged her stump of a tail.

Dr. Perkins gave her another two "locals," shots to kill the pain in her feet as he sewed up her paws. Then Mom put John in the tent on top of our extra sleeping bag, tightened the Velco straps on her doggie coat then covered her with a blanket. John sighed deeply and closed her eyes.

"Well," the doctor said as he inspected Happy's paws, "these are deep punctures and I can't sew them. You need to keep her still and her feet clean until they heal. I can wash them, but you need to get some antibiotics into both dogs when you get home."

Right, I thought. Happy would go nuts sitting in a crate. I thought about how we'd manage to keep her off her feet until they healed. Maybe we could wrap them with tape and let her walk around.

"Thanks," Mom said.

"I've never treated an animal before," he said.

"What kind of doctor are you?" I asked him.

"Pediatrician. I deal with kids."

"That's good enough," I told him.

"Okay Tuli," Mom said. "Get your stuff."

"Why? Now what?"

"Hasty search. It may rain and I want to get back out there one more time before dark. It's going to be cold. Grab both your packs."

She walked over to tell Rowdy to watch the dogs and to keep them warm. Then we went to the Operations desk. Mom leaned over and pointed on the map. "We're going back here," she told me and Mickey. "Down 255. I need an ATV. A bigger one with a bench behind the driver."

"Can't you take Rowdy's dogs?" Mickey asked.

"No." I knew Mom wouldn't tell him that Cosmo growled. Instead she said, "They're used to Rowdy. They'll probably keep trying to come back to camp. Too much of a chance to take. And if they don't act right, then I'm stuck out there with them."

"You can take my machine," a big, burley guy with a foot-long beard said. He was overweight although his ATV looked lean and ready to go.

Mom eyed his Arctic Cat 500 outfitted with a ton of hunting accessories. "Thanks," Mom said.

I jogged back to the tent to get my gear. For some reason that I couldn't explain later, I also grabbed the hunk of roast from the food chest. By this time of the cold day the meat didn't need ice. I grabbed several potatoes and a pack of smoked salmon to go with the Beenie Weenies, corn and other items already in my pack. I knew Mom would scold me for taking such heavy food on a quick search. But my female intuition tried to tell me something and I refused to ignore it. I could always put the items back when we returned.

After I gave Happy a pat on the head and the sleeping John a kiss on the nose, I ran to meet Mom.

"Where have you been?" She asked impatiently. Her eyes were red and she looked like she'd been crying.

"I had to get my packs like you said. What's wrong?"

"Nothing."

"You're crying."

Mom paused and looked the other direction while she wiped away more tears. "Tuli," she said firmly, "I didn't find the men. And my dogs got injured."

"That was an accident," I said. "And you can't expect to find who you're looking for right away."

"I usually do."

"Mom," I started. But before I could say that she tries too hard to be superwoman she interrupted.

"Get on," she ordered.

"You'll find them, Mother."

She didn't reply.

We put our gear on the shelf behind me. Mom clicked the machine into gear with her foot then pressed the accelerator with her thumb. We left a spray of wet dirt behind us. I wanted to yell 'Yee Haw!' but knew she wouldn't like that. Mom shifted gears and flew over bumps in the road so fast that my rear came off the seat and my leg repeatedly hit the rifle boot.

My mother knew exactly where to go. After less than fifteen minutes she stopped and got off. We took our fanny packs and larger shoulder packs from the metal basket on the back of the ATV.

"I'm going to walk east for thirty minutes. You go west. Then come back. Got it?"

"Yes, I got it."

"This is a quick search, so don't go wandering around. Got your compass?"

"Okay, Mom. Geez."

"You did study the map, didn't you?"

"Yes Mom. All day. I stayed at the table all day, you know."

"All right. This ground is hard to walk on in places. It's steep and pine needles cover up holes. Be back here in one hour, exactly. *Anukfoka?*-Got it?"

"*Ah*-Yes.. I already said that I got it."

We turned and went our separate ways.

"Tulip!" Mom yelled from fifty feet away.

I slowly turned to see what else she had to say.

"Be careful. *Chi hullo li*-I love you."

There was no use in trying to figure out why Mom got mad then thought better of it and said something nice to make up for snapping at me. So I waved and turned back to the way I was headed.

As I walked with my eyes scanning the ground, I gritted my teeth and thought about the day.

Let's see. I'd kept a grown man from breaking down until rescuers arrived to take care of his friend. I rounded up the rescuers, in fact. Then I found someone to go find Mom, Rowdy and the injured dogs. And I had made camp the night before.

Man, I was tired already and I hadn't even been out searching. Dad said to do my best and I sure was trying.

Anyway, the shadows in the forest deepened and out of the corner of my eye I thought I saw a track almost covered by leaves. Maybe it was the edge of a footprint. I got closer, moved the leaves and looked at it from one angle, then from another. Deer hoof.

I saw a flash through the trees. The storm was coming from the south. I counted to determine how far away lighting might be. *Acuffa, tuklo, tuchina* . . . Then thunder boomed. That meant three miles away. Mom taught me that if you count after you see light from the lightning, then you'd know how far away the lightning could be. One second equals one mile. I count in Choctaw because each count has to be one second apart and I speak more slowly in Choctaw.

Well, no matter which way of counting proved to be the most accurate, rain would be here soon. I'd already crossed two small streams created by the previous rain, an illegal mini-dump with a tire, car battery, clothes and beer cans. I'd been to the abrupt end of one neglected dirt road that dropped off into a deep valley and passed dozens of downed trees from a long-ago fire.

I felt a raindrop on my cheek. Oh great. I looked up and saw heavy clouds directly over head. I was going to be wet and uncomfortable.

Then I looked down and saw a perfect left footprint. The heel of the size eleven boot had a notch cut out of it. Then I saw a right foot, then a left foot. To the sides of that set of prints were two other large ones and then a smaller set. Three men and one child.

The tracks were easy to see. At least they were easy for me to see. Not everyone pays attention to the small clues that are all around them. If you know what tracks belong to what animals, your hike in the woods can be a lot more fun.

I had always wanted to learn to track and I wanted to be good at it. I'm just like Mom in that respect. I'm ready to work hard, wear myself out and do things that will get me in trouble.

"Learning to track is hard work, Tuli," Mom told me. "If you're a good tracker, that means you have spent many hours looking at footprints in various kinds of ground cover: sand, clay, dirt, cinders, and all the above covered with brush. So let's work on it."

And we did.

We looked at tracks at all times of the day. "The sun can either help or make it more difficult," she told me. "See, if you look down at a track when the sun is directly over your head, you won't see the print easily unless it's deep. If we track when the sun is either coming up or going down, then the edges of the print will leave a shadow and is more obvious."

So we looked at tracks in the morning and in the evening.

"Good trackers often are able to tell how old the track is, depending on the climate, the debris around the track, and moisture. Like this turkey track." She pointed at it with her toe. "It's a day old. The dirt around the edges have fallen in some."

Then we looked at books with pictures of shoe soles.

"Good trackers study catalogues that show the soles of running, hiking and walking shoes so they can identify shoes. This is important since friends and family sometimes recall what kind of shoes the lost person wears." Then she made me identify the soles of her shoes. I had never paid attention to shoe bottoms before. I sure have after that.

"But Tuli, remember that footprints aren't the only evidence left by a passing person. Broken trees limbs, crushed grass, smashed animal poop, even scuff marks on rocks are all there if you know what to look for. If you're not observant then you may not see anything, except by accident." Then she stepped on some coyote scat. "See, I made a partial print of my sole in the scat."

So yes, it helps to live in the middle of a lot of trees so one can be outside a lot. I listen to forest noises everyday. I can tell the difference between normal outdoor sounds and those noises that I need to pay attention to. Like no sounds at all, which might mean a predator is hanging around, or maybe another person is nearby.

Some of my friends who camp with me get scared at hearing crows, ravens and hawks fly. Their wings sound like swooshing and unless you know what the noise is you might think it's a large animal breathing.

Come to think of it, Shawn gets scared when we hike in the thick woods. Once, after he almost stepped on a big garter snake out by the Anadarko Mountains I had to talk to him real quietly like I sometimes do with Pete so he wouldn't start crying. I hadn't thought about that much before now. I wondered how Shawn would act in this situation. Then I wondered how Arnie Anapatubbee and Jen Wilson would like being out here. Since neither one of them ever wanted to go camping with me, I considered that they're afraid of the woods.

I surprised myself. It occurred to me that the people I usually worried about liking me weren't important right now. I pushed them out of my mind then looked to the south and saw that the feet had followed a game trail. Then the feet branched off right in front of me. No wonder I hadn't seen them until now. Clearly, the feet were headed towards another thin game trail.

What struck me as strange was how the four sets of tracks zig-zagged through the trees. They had covered a lot of ground, but as far as I could tell, they didn't go in a straight line very often. They'd head one way, then cut at a sharp angle to go another way, then sometimes backtrack. Deer walked in straighter lines than these guys.

More rain. Then a huge burst of thunder. I put on my rain slicker that was designed to cover me and my pack. It reached to my knees. My boots were supposed to be waterproof, so for the moment I stayed dry.

I hadn't been paying attention to where I was going. I looked at my watch then realized I had wandered around for 45 minutes.

The rain fell harder. As I turned to go back the way I came, big drops began to fall in a torrent, a blinding gray waterfall that kept me from seeing ten feet ahead. Should I stay put so Mom could find me? Or, should I try and backtrack? With the rain falling hard I couldn't be certain sure about my position.

Deep thunder boomed in the distance. As long as lightning stays away from me, I don't mind being in the rain. In fact, running in warm Oklahoma rain is one of my favorite things to do. On the other hand I'm really scared of getting hit by lightning. Then a sharp peel made me jump.

I used to be afraid of storms. But my grandmother told me something that I always remember when a storm comes through. My mother's mom is Jaunty Asatubbe, a thin, colorful lady who lightens up a room when she walks in. She has a huge garden on her allotment that she uses to grow almost all the food she eats. She's got milk goats, chickens, ducks, geese, turkeys and peacocks that wander around her property under the protection of her two big white dogs.

Once when Pete and I spent the night at her clean, plant-filled house a summer storm came through. Lightning crashed and we saw a bolt hit one of her pecan trees out back and knock off a huge branch.

"Don't be afraid of the storm," she told us. She stood at the upstairs bedroom window and had a big grin on her face like she was enjoying the thunder and raindrops that pelted the roof like gunshots. "This is the way it's supposed to be. We need the rain to help the land live and grow right. A harsh bolt of *malahta* starts fires that clear out the dead wood in the forests. The noise is the way lightning tells us that it has arrived."

"So lightning is talking to us?" Pete asked with big eyes. He pulled the blanket up to his chin and peeked out.

"Sure. You can't be afraid of it Petie. But you have to respect it. Let it do what the Creator *Hashtali* intended."

Jaunty told me many other things that gave me comfort when I was in the woods. Spiders, snakes, coyotes all have a place and they have to be allowed to behave they way they're supposed to. "Admire them and respect them, Tuli," she told me. "Look at the beautiful webs *chulhkan* weaves. See how *sinti* moves silently through the grass without arms or legs and eats the mice. There are too many mice. The gray *Nashoba holba* and his tall ears hide in the tall grass and sees everything. Don't be afraid of them. They deserve to be here."

I remember Jaunty's words, but I mainly remember the smile she has when she talks about animals and nature. Things that might seem scary to some people are no longer scary to me. Lightning is one of them.

Then I heard something odd. Two loud booms, only one second apart. It didn't really sound like thunder, although I couldn't be certain because of the heavy rain. I thought that maybe the lost men were shooting their rifles. That can be a good idea to attract attention, but not in the rain when the searchers can't hear them.

I took the storm whistle out from my shirt where it hung from a thin chain. I covered my ears with my hands and blew several times. The shrill whistle is supposed to be heard over a hurricane, but since I could barely hear the rifle shots I doubted that anyone could hear my whistle through this storm.

So, I needed to decide what to do about shelter. The lightning made up my mind for me. You're not supposed to stand under a tree when it's lightning, but I wasn't about to stand out in the open, either. I thought that a pine tree shorter than the others around it wouldn't be a target for lightning. That's not really true, you know, but it also had thick branches that would serve as a roof while the soft pile of pine needles below me might drain well.

I piled up a bunch of needles then pulled my tarp and a large plastic garbage bag out of my pack. I put the garbage bag over my head; I had cut a hole for my head to go through like a smart person should, then wrapped the tarp around me. Before long I sat huddled within my tarp, feeling cold, tired and damp. It's a good thing I've never been afraid of the dark or of night time.

"It's a part of the day cycle," Jaunty said when I was very small and concerned about what might be in my dark closet at night. "Day comes then night comes. Long ago we didn't have electricity for night lights and televisions. We slept better when it was very dark. You should sleep the best outside where there are only the stars and the moon for light."

Thanks to Jaunty, I always feel comforted by night. Each day, when the sun starts to go down, my body relaxes and my mind calms. Unless I have a pain like in my broken leg, I sleep well. Then when the sun comes up, my eyes open and I'm rested. That's the way it should be.

Even though it was growing darker and I should have been peaceful, but I worried about what Mom was doing. I took out my walkie talkie and as I pressed the talk button, my stomach flipped. My poor guts worked over time these days.

No sound. No static, nothing. I had forgotten to change out the batteries! This is without question a major mistake on my part. Mom taught me to change out the batteries every six months, more if I used the machine. I forgot to change them about a month ago. No use worrying about that now. No batteries in the forest.

I heard a branch snap. I sat up and looked out from under my tarp and saw no movement. Still, my heart beat fast and I wondered what could have made a branch break. A coyote? Would *nashoba holba* be out in such weather? I doubted it. They're pretty clever and like to be comfortable. I kept looking and still nothing moved. I shined my strong flashlight all around and saw nothing but heavy rain.

Then I had a thought that made me gasp. When I was small, Jaunty told me about *shampes*, those big hairy, smelly man-creatures that are supposed to be like Big Foot or an abominable snowman. His feet are huge and supposedly people can smell them from a long way off. I sniffed and smelled nothing but damp pine needles and pine wood.

Now, I know in my heart that there's no way a *shampe* could be here on the North Rim because he only hangs around southern Oklahoma and is out of his territory. In fact, there's a group of people there called the "Oklahoma Monkey Chasers" who spend much of their time looking for him. Even a movie called "The Boggy Creek Monster" was based on our *shampe* legend.

This is the kind of thing that gets my imagination working. Sometimes too much. Growing up with an imaginative mother and grandmother, plus a little brother who wants to believe in monsters and fairies, has given me a mind that can create all kinds of situations and creatures.

I shined my light again and jumped when a small branch fell. It made the same noise that I heard before, so evidently that's what startled me in the first place. As my breathing slowed, I thought about the other creatures my mother thinks are real.

There also are stories about *Nalusa Falaya*, a dark thing that lures hunters away from their campfires and into the woods and are never seen again. I always wondered how that story got passed around if the hunters are lured away. I mean, how could they tell us what happened if they disappeared? Mom swears she saw it once. She told my dad that it looked a ninja and had red eyes. She felt like she should follow it, but she resisted. Dad said she was worn out from a long day of tracking and was imagining things.

Then there's *Kashhotapolo* who's part-man and part-deer. The only people who see him are hunters who are alone. Hunters bravely talk about *Kashhotapolo* when they're in a group because they know it won't appear unless they're by themselves. I shined my light around once more just to make sure he wasn't around. After all, there was no one else around me. I was alone.

I took two deep breaths. No *Kashhotapol.* No *shampe.* And no *Nalusa Falaya.*

What would these creatures be doing on the North Rim, anyway? I reached into my coat, under my sweater and long underwear to find my medicine bundle. My great-great uncle Leroy Bear Red Ears gave it to me a few years ago when he did a ceremony for me and Mom. I had been with my mother when she found two women that had been carried off by a tornado. Their bodies lay in dirty creek water that ran through the allotment of a

Choctaw family. Because we had touched the dead women, we had to be cleansed. After praying and singing, Uncle Leroy gave me a bundle and told me to always wear it.

"It will protect you," he said.

"From everything?" I asked.

"No, of course not," he laughed, his blue-bead necklace tinkling as he tossed his head back. "But if you use your head, stay away from danger and think good thoughts, then it will make sure you're safe."

Well, to me that sounded like I was the one who would take care of me, but I wasn't going to argue with him. Besides, I think he was trying to teach me a lesson about responsibility and making wise decisions.

I sighed as I tucked my bundle back into my clothes, stretched then dozed off under my tarp.

As I faded, I thought that I should have paid closer attention to the time. And I should have changed the batteries to the walkie-talkie.

My leg throbbed and I hoped that hiking was a good workout since I couldn't run. How much would my training suffer while I was out here? Would I get out of shape?

The rain tapped on my tarp as I fell asleep.

Chapter 7: By Myself

I woke up because a stick poked into the back of my neck. Even though the temperature was cold, my cozy nest felt fairly comfortable under my tarp. After all, I was insulated with long underwear, heavy outer clothes, a plastic bag over my torso, plus a tarp and a bunch of ground litter piled on top of it all.

A squirrel chattered at me from a low branch of my pine tree. The way the little guy carried on told me that he was probably surprised to see me emerge from the ground like a big bear wearing clothes.

"*Halito fani*-Hi squirrel." I clucked to him and he stopped to consider me for a few seconds, then skittered up the tree and disappeared out of sight.

I looked around at the still forest and the grey clouds above me. The air felt very cold and made me cough when I took in a deep breath.

Trying to keep my spirits up, I said, "*Himak nittak achukma*-It's a nice day." As Jaunty has told me repeatedly, every day, even a freezing one, is a nice day.

I shook away the pine needles, rolled up my tarp and took off my plastic bag. I swallowed a swig of water and ate a chewy granola bar. After I flossed, blew my nose and wiped off my face and hands with an always-handy diaper wipe. I put my warm groves back on as I looked around for the tracks I saw the evening before. They were gone, although the game trail used by deer this early morning looked even more obvious after the rain had darkened the dirt.

My pack felt heavier this morning than it did the night before, so I tightened the waist band. Some hikers prefer that their shoulders handle most of the weight, I but I do better with the weight on my hips.

While adjusting my straps, I saw movement through the tree trunks. Then I heard a huff. Most of my friends who have hiked with me are surprised at hearing a deer snort. If you're quiet and upwind from a deer, you can hear them breathe. Deer are very difficult to ambush on foot. That's why rifle hunters use scopes and hide in blinds.

The small herd of white tailed does stood still for a moment, then bounded off fifty feet, stopped, looked at me again, then ran away down the game trail that went in straight lines for the most part, with a few juts to avoid oak groves and large rocks.

What should I do now? Mom's lessons echoed in my brain. "Not only are you supposed to inspect the ground in front of you, Tuli," she told me just this summer, "you're also supposed to look off to the sides. You have to look on branches of trees and bushes for pieces of clothing that may have been ripped off. And you also should look behind yourself periodically."

I stopped and looked behind me.

"Tuli, pay attention to me. You also have to listen carefully." A few years ago Mom found a lost Boy Scout with laryngitis and a sprained ankle. He continually hit two rocks together to make noise because he didn't know how to whistle. Mom found him sitting on a rock with no injuries other than sunburn.

If you search like you're supposed to, it's a stressful and very tiring activity. If a lost person walks four miles then he or she could be anywhere within 50 square miles. If that person has gone ten miles, then the area expands to 314 square miles. That's a lot of territory to cover.

Because there's no time to waste in a search, Mom taught me to be aggressive in hunting for the lost person. That means looking in bushes, behind logs and among rock piles. Once, Mom found an unconscious hunter buried under a pile of leaves. His camouflage helped him blend into the environment, but Mom had noticed that the pile of leaves looked more like a lump. She investigated and after a two-day stay in the hospital for hypothermia, the hunter was home in time for Thanksgiving dinner.

So by order of Mom, I looked all around me, behind me, among the downed branches and behind logs and big rocks. I found nothing except the deer tracks in front of me. But I had a thought: yesterday the weather had been clear in the morning, so if the lost hunters planned to walk, then why didn't they follow the sun towards the west, or at least use it as a point of reference to go straight? The tracks I saw last night before the rain wiped them out revealed that they headed towards the game trail.

If the hunters were confused and scared then following an established game trail might make them feel more secure. Animals always know where they're going. And even if the deer's destination isn't the same as men's, sometimes lost people think they're following a leader deer or a rancher's cow who will take them to civilization.

Mom's voice echoed again. "You have to look on branches of trees and bushes for pieces of clothing that may have been ripped off," she said. I decided to follow the game trail to see if there were signs that the men went this way.

I hadn't gone ten feet when I recalled Mom's advice. I stopped and looked behind me. Then I saw a small piece of silver half buried in the dirt. A bird bolted up in surprise from the brush when I yelled with happiness at finding a sign. I picked up the small silver item, wiped the mud off and realized that I had discovered a very new gum wrapper.

I reckoned that someone had dropped it then another person who walked behind him ground the wrapper into the mud. Normally I'd be annoyed at someone who pollutes, but since this was a clear sign that at least two humans had come this way, I'd forgive him.

An hour later I came across a hunter's camp set back off a dirt road. I recalled that this must be road 255B and Mickey had said that these men had not seen the lost hunters. Well, no one was home now. It's pretty common during hunting season for hunters to set up camp then stay out all day looking for game. At the North Rim, it's a sure bet that your stuff is safe from thieves. Aside from me, that is.

This looked like a nicely-furnished camp, with an expensive four-door truck with an expensive camping trailer attached to it and another big truck with a large trailer that probably toted three or four ATVs.

"Nice ride," I said to the truck.

Four folding chairs sat around a camping table. Three ice chests were placed under an awning. Two fancy camping tents stood next to a tall, narrow tent that may have been a portable outhouse.

I looked inside the tents to find three sleeping bags in each one. The fire circle still smoldered, a real no-no in any forest, but especially in a forest that has suffered droughts, even if it had rained the night before.

A dressed doe hung from a tree by a chain, the game bag wrapped around her.

"Sorry *issi*," I said to the headless body as I touched her flank. I know that there are enough deer on the North Rim to survive the hunting seasons, but I still can't bear the thought of killing one. I looked at the tag taped to her hind leg. The name Robert Parson. Not that his name would do me any good, although I was for some reason comforted that I knew it.

The does' head sat on top of a piece of thick cardboard in the ATV trailer. If hunters kill a deer, he or she has to provide the head so the rangers know what gender of deer they took. If you're only allowed to take a doe, then you better only have a doe and not a buck. And vice versa.

One of the ice chests was filled with soda and beer cans, plus small orange juice containers so I took two of those. I drank one and put the other in my fanny pack. There were several dozen cold sandwiches in another chest and I took two, in addition to a candy bar and a small bag of pretzels.

I opened one sandwich bag and smelled tuna fish. The other was cheese and mayonnaise. Neither are my first choices, but after a long day in the woods I'll eat almost anything that's normal. That is, no bugs, raw fish or other things like that.

Mom says that Choctaws a long time ago would dry-out corn kernels with hickory smoke, partly to preserve the corn and also to keep insects from eating it. So when Choctaws went out to hunt they carried a bag of either cracked corn with them or finely ground corn to mix with water to soften the hard corn. That sounds pretty awful to me. Mom said they preferred it with the more tasty milk and honey, which sounds better. Some Choctaws like to argue that we created Corn Flakes. I like that part of the story.

Who wants to eat hard corn when in the woods all day, getting tired and very hungry? Traditional foods like *nita*-bears, *hachunchuba*-alligators, *koinchush*-wildcats, or *koichus*-panthers are not my idea of yummy meals, either. I'll eat most fruits and vegetables anytime, though.

Jaunty grows the Three Sisters in her garden, that is, the three vegetables known as corn, squash and green beans. Many tribes grew these three together because the beans vines climb the corn stalks, while the big squash leaves provide shade and help retain moisture. And, growing them together creates growth so thick that it keeps out deer and other animals. Jaunty cooks up all three in the frying pan and mixes them with tomatoes, red peppers and garlic. Add a bit of soy sauce and I can eat a huge bowl filled with yellow, green and red colors.

"I'd give almost anything for a bowl of squash and peppers,"

I said aloud.

Obviously there is no squash growing around the North Rim so I'd have to find something else. Now, before you think I approve of stealing other people's food, I don't. But, if you're stuck out in the middle of the North Rim of the Grand Canyon looking for lost people and being somewhat disoriented (you notice I did not say "lost") you might start to worry about yourself. Like I was starting to do.

To explain my theft, I told myself that the hunters had a deer hanging from a tree, which meant they had enough food in case they had a problem. Judging from the numerous antennae jutting up from their trucks I knew that they had plenty means of communication. And transportation. These people were prepared.

I took a five dollar bill from my fanny pack and left it under a rock under one of the chests. Next to that I placed a note written on my tiny notebook paper telling them who I was. I told them what I was doing and why, and asked them to please contact the rangers, the local Jacob Lake Lodge-anyone actually, because they'd take that information to the authorities-to inform them that at 10:00 this day, at least, I was in the area and okay.

I thought about waiting around for the hunters to return, but I also knew that obsessed hunters often stay out all day and into the night. If six people were in camp and only one got a deer then I bet myself that the group would stay out until the other guys bagged a few more animals.

So, I continued my search. "Thanks guys," I said as I walked away from the comfort and security of their camp.

I picked up the game trail then lost the tracks when I ran into a grove of oak trees. Dead, dry leaves covered the ground and I was forced to walk around the perimeter of the thick grove before I found the trail again.

After another thirty minutes I found their tracks on a dirt road, one of the forest roads that feature pot holes, washboards and various other hazards. This may have been Forest Road 417 or maybe 218, one of those "fingers" Mickey told us about. I should have brought a map. No use getting mad at myself over that. My pea brain had enough to worry about. I easily followed the tracks for about a mile, when they turned off back into the forest.

"Now why go back into the woods when you have a road?" I asked aloud. My leg ached and I reached down to gently rub the spot below my knee where the bone had snapped almost six months before.

Then I followed the tracks up a slight hill. At the top, the footprints were jumbled, as if the men had wandered around while trying to get their bearings. On the rise where I stood, the cold wind increased and the lack of trees made it easy for me to see that the clouds were building. If a snow storm was coming like the Hot Shot Lucy predicted, then my situation could get serious very fast. The lost men needed to get back to Operations.

The tracks went back down the other side of the slope and I followed. As I neared a large, long-dead decaying log, something on the ground on top of one of the branches from that dead tree caught my eye: a patch of red. I put my gloved hand to the spot, touched it, then smelled it. Blood. I looked around to see if there was more and I saw none.

There were no animal tracks anywhere, so it wasn't a wounded deer.

"Someone's hurt," I said to the trees.

"Caw, caw," a large shiny black raven called.

"*Halito Fala chito*," I greeted. Some Indians are scared when they see crows and ravens, but I think they're smart and have something to say. Of course, you have to speak their language and I didn't. But I could speak English and Choctaw so hopefully the raven could pick up a few words of what I said.

I looked back to the trail. Since the blood hadn't gelled I knew the hunters had to be close. I continued to follow the trail then came to another log. The feet shuffled around again and continued on their way. I noticed that to the side of the foot print wearing the boot with a notch in the sole was a hole. Every time that foot took a step, the small hole with a circumference of a dime appeared. A crutch, I figured. Probably made from a branch.

"Someone else is hurt," I said to *Fala chito*, who hopped from one branch to another, until she reached a branch that overlooked a valley. She cawed once then flew away. I thought that she needed to satisfy her curiosity about me, but as I reached the edge of the small valley, I looked down and saw four figures dressed in green. I smiled and took off at a slow jog to reach them.

"Hey!" I yelled. They all turned around. Judging from their expressions, I might have been an alien dropped from the sky.

I got closer to them and asked, "Any of you Mr. Wabash? Mr. Martin? The Johnstons?"

The largest man cursed then put his hands on his hips. "Yeah, that's us."

They all looked dirty, tired and stressed. All perked up and kept looking behind me, up the hill like they thought the troops were coming to save them.

"Are you it?" The big man with the cowboy hat and ponytail asked me. The top of a tattoo showed above his collar on his neck. I wondered what it looked like and if it also covered his chest.

"It what?"

"You got a cell phone?" One of the others asked.

"No." They continued to look at me. "My mom and I did a quick search last night," I said, "and we didn't take our phones." I didn't mention the walkie-talkie battery problem.

"Your *mom?*" The cowboy asked, like it was the weirdest thing he'd ever heard.

"That's right."

"And you didn't bring phones? That's smart," said the big man.

"Cell phones don't work on the Rim."

"Says who?"

I ignored that. Mom, however, would have jumped on him like a duck on a June bug.

"Anyone got a GPS?"

"GPS? What's that?"

"Never mind. Y'all okay?"

"For the most part," he answered. "I got a sprained ankle and it hurts like all get out." His long hair tied back with a rubber band was a mess of snarls and I felt an urge to comb it.

"What's your name?"

"I'm Stan Wabash," he said as he breathed hard. Like it took effort to talk. "That's Frank Martin and Jody and Jody Johnston."

"Jody and Jody?"

"Yeah. That's our name," answered Mr. Johnston.

Well, that's weird. Both father and son have the same name. I mean, I know that happens, but usually people call one Jr. or something. They looked very much alike, almost like brothers. They were tall and thin and had reddish hair. Their fair skin had already been burned after several days outside without sunscreen.

The boy's chin was dark red, almost maroon. His unzipped coat and the front of his camouflage shirt looked to be the same color. "What happened to you?" I asked.

"Spilt his lip," Big Jody said.

I reached into my fanny pack and found my tube of Neosporin. I walked over to the kid. "Jody?"

He looked at me with swollen eyes, like he'd been crying. I saw that his dried blood also covered his neck.

"Where did y'all spend the night last night?" I asked.

"We found a hole in the side of one of these valleys," Mr. Johnston said.

"You call that a hole?" answered Mr. Wabash. "It was more of bowl. The wind and rain hit us all night."

"We d-d-did pretty well with the tarp, though," Mr. Martin added.

"Did any of you fire your rifle last night?" I asked.

"We a-a-all did," answered Mr. Martin. "I used up all m-m-my ammo." I had never heard an adult stutter before. He was big and burly and the stutter and quiet tone didn't match his large looks.

"Us too," said Mr. Johnston, nodding towards his child.

"The last two shots around eleven were mine," said Mr. Wabash. "So you heard us?"

"Barely and through the rain. No one else heard you, though."

"Is th-th-that how you f-f-found us?" Mr. Martin asked in his quiet voice.

"No. I found your tracks."

"How'd you know to look for us in the first place?" Little Jody asked. His lip was deeply split, swollen and needed stitches. Other than that, he was kind of cute, like that boy in Spy Kids.

"Because we came from Oklahoma to help find you. I mean, I just came along."

"Ok-a-la-homa?" Mr. Martin slowly asked. His cheeks were chapped and he'd be hurting tonight. "Wh-wh-what are you doing way out h-h-here?"

"The search and rescue teams around Flagstaff are already looking for a lost child. A Utah group is out looking for you, but they only have a few people. The forest rangers are searching too. There aren't many of them, either."

"You l-l-look for lost people much?" Mr. Martin asked. I knew that he asked me that question to find out if I knew what I was doing.

"Well, the Oklahoma group doesn't get a lot of business if you compare us to the mountain, desert and big forest areas. Southern hurricane rescue is covered by the Houston or Dallas SRDA. Lost people and bad guys like drug smugglers in the southwest deserts get chased by the Albuquerque unit with help from the Border Patrol. Avalanches are covered by the Washington State, Oregon and Vermont units."

"So what do you do in your Oklahoma . . . Unit?" Mr. Wabash asked in a sarcastic voice. "Anything?"

Mr. Martin coughed and I hoped it was just to clear his throat and not because he was getting sick. If he was getting sick he needed to wait until he got home. He bent down and rubbed his knee. He was the one with the knee replacement.

If Mom were here, she'd really let Mr. Wise Guy Wabash have it. But Mom wasn't here. I was. So I sighed then tried to explain. "They often have to search for victims of tornadoes who are sometimes carried miles from their homes. Oklahoma is filled with deer, turkeys, quail and other animals. Oklahoma has lots of prairies and thick forests. Most of Mom's jobs focus on finding lost hunters. The McAlester Sheriff's Posse is pretty much a partner with our McAlester SAR unit and so . . ."

"T-t-tornadoes?" asked Mr. Martin. "C-c-can you live through that?" He sounded like the kids Mom talks to at school about her search work. They all want to know if you could be sucked up by winds going hundreds of miles an hour and then be gently put back on the ground.

"No." That was all I cared to talk about it. Finding the victims of tornadoes is about as ugly a job as you can have.

"So, uh," Mr. Martin started again. He really wanted to know.

Instead of answering I looked at Jody, the son of Jody. "You cut your lip falling over a log?"

"Yeah. I tripped on a branch. How'd you know that?"

"I saw your blood," I answered.

Mr. Wabash cleared his throat. Then the big man limped closer. Despite the crutch he heavily favored his left leg. "So where are they?" He glanced around like he thought the rescue team might burst out of the woods. I smelled harsh breath.

"Not far. Maybe three miles north." I squeezed out a glob of Neosporin. "Here Jody, put this on your lip. Try not to lick it off. You need a stitch to close that. If Mom were here she could do it."

"When are they coming?" Mr. Wabash repeated. He breathed hard. You notice he said "they" and not "she."

"They may not come," I said. "The rain last night wiped out your tracks. I just got lucky in picking up your trail a few miles ago. It's getting cold and it's hard for the dogs to smell you."

"You mean they got dogs looking for us?" Mr. Wabash sounded angry.

"Yup."

He let out a curse.

I was right. He was angry. But more importantly, his pride was bruised. Just like Mom had predicted. "Dogs can't smell in the cold? Why not?"

"Of course they can. But it gets harder the colder it gets. Even with those stinky socks of yours." I looked at Little Jody and when he tried to smile his cut opened and blood spurted onto my coat.

"Sorry," he muttered. His face turned red with embarrassment.

"Now everyone might know we're lost." Mr. Wabash snorted through his nose.

"Everyone does know," I corrected. "Why didn't you just stay where you were? How come you're wandering around?"

He answered in a confident voice. "Because I know where we are and I know how to get us back."

I looked at Jody Jr., then at his father. "Mr. Johnston, you should have stayed in one place. You can't drag your son all over the North Rim."

"I thought I knew where we were, too," he answered weakly. He kept his hands in his pockets. He shivered and that was not a good thing. From this looks of his thin neck, he didn't have much insulation. Body fat, that is.

"There's a storm coming. Can you feel it getting colder?"

"I can," Little Jody said.

"We need to get in a safe place," I said.

"Oh no, we're not," answered Mr. Wabash. "We have to keep moving and get back to camp." He wheezed, and along with him being overweight I felt a twinge of fear that he might have a heart attack right out in the middle of the woods. I know CPR, but sometimes that's not enough to save a person unless an ambulance is on the way.

"Mr. Wabash, your camp is not in the direction you're headed."

"Look, little girl," he said as he hobbled closer to me. My heart beat faster and I held my breath, but I stood straight and didn't back up any. "We know what we're doing and we're going to keep walking."

"You're limping," I said.

"Yeah, so what? I been hurt worse."

"We need to sit still so Mom can find us," I repeated. It became clear that repetition wasn't going to impact this guy's thinking.

"Your mom?" Asked Mr. Wabash.

"Yeah. She's an expert tracker."

He laughed at that.

"She always finds who she's looking for."

"She didn't find us."

"Our tracking dogs got cut up by barbed wire yesterday and last night my mom and I got separated. It rained and your tracks are gone."

"I'm not waiting for some woman to come get me," Mr. Wabash insisted. "We gotta get outta here." His wheeze got louder. "We can't die out here."

"I ran into a hunters' camp about two miles that way." I pointed north.

"Why didn't they come with you?" Mr. Wabash asked with another wheeze and a cough. He sounded like a smoker and I wished he'd blow his nose. How come some people can't even feel that they should clean their gunky noses? I took off my glove and felt my nose. Just in case.

"I left a note telling them to contact the authorities that I had gotten this far. You all can sit still while I go back and get them. They can drive over the ridge and pick us up."

Mr. Wabash fidgeted. "I'd rather not," he said.

"Why?"

"Because I want to get back to base camp by myself."

"I can understand that," I said. "But, you're not by yourself."

Well, at least I could understand it from his perspective. Here stood a macho man who felt embarrassed to be lost. He didn't know the location of base camp which was why he led the group deeper into the forest. He wanted to get out of the mess alone. Unfortunately, he didn't understand my viewpoint.

"You have to get Jody Jr. out of here." Surely, I thought, that would make sense.

"Jody," Mr. Wabash corrected. "There's no 'Jr.'"

"It's okay, Stan," Big Jody said in my defense.

"We'll get him out," Mr. Wabash said.

"You're limping really bad," I said. "You're not going to die out here. We have everything we need to stay in one place for days if we have to. But we don't have to."

I glanced at Baby Jody and his lip. Man, it looked bad. It was swollen up like a burl on a tree trunk.

"You hungry, Jody?"

"Yeah," said Big and Little Jody at the same time.

"Y'all have food?" I asked. I figured not.

"N-n-not much," answered Mr. Martin.

I took out the cheese sandwich and handed it to Small Jody. He took the white bread and American slice then gobbled it faster than my dogs eat their dinner. "I have some corn chips and two candy bars."

Mr. Martin and Mr. Johnston, that is, Big Jody, took the food and started eating. Had they not eaten anything lately? Mr. Johnston shook his head no. Mr. Martin somehow got chocolate in his moustache.

"The weather's about to turn bad," I said. I looked up and through the tree branches and saw the clouds blowing around.

"Then we need to get moving," said Mr. Wabash.

"Wait a sec," I said. "You need to stay here and I'll go."

"Oh no, you won't go," he said. "We'll all go. Come on you guys."

I sighed and tried once more. This was like training dogs. Or kindergartners. "Mr. Wabash, I can be back at that camp in an hour. I can get a truck here in another fifteen minutes. I'm not as tired as you are."

"Who said I was tired? And who says you can find it again?" And then he took off at a fast limp, his followers behind him.

Chapter 8: Nashoba Lusa

"What's your n-n-name?" Mr. Martin asked me as we hiked in front of the hobbling Mr. Wabash. I had taken the lead and went slow, knowing that for all his posturing and bluster, Mr. Bad Ponytail struggled to keep up.

"Tuli Black Wolf," I answered. I knew from experience that the next thing they'd ask was if I'm Indian.

"You an Indian?"

The first thing I want to do whenever anyone asks me that is to be a smart mouth. I mean, I have dark skin, long dark hair, dark eyes and my last name is Black Wolf. I certainly don't look Swedish. Mom always tells me I'd be rude not to just say "I'm Chahta."

"Yeah," I told him. "Actually, I'm Chahta."

"N-n-never heard of that tribe," Mr. Martin said.

"You may know it as Choctaw. We originated in Mississippi and along with other tribes who lived in the Southeast, like the Cherokees, Chickasaws, Creeks and Seminoles, we were moved in the 1830s to Indian Territory. President Andrew Jackson moved us so white settlers could take our land. Lots of other tribes from around the country were moved there, too. At one time there were almost seventy tribes in Indian Territory. It's Oklahoma now."

"Oh, yeah. How c-c-come you say Choctaw different?"

"Because that's what Chahtas call themselves. Like Navajos out here call themselves Dineh, but you all call them Navajos. Winnebagos call themselves Ho Chunks. Cherokees are Tsalagis or Aniyunwea. Creeks are Muscogees. The list goes on."

"That's confusing," said Mr. Wabash.

"Not to us."

No one said anything to that.

"Oklahoma comes from two Choctaw words. *Okla* means man and *humma* is red."

"Wow, cool," Jody Jr. burbled through his fat lip.

I reached into my fanny pack and felt around. The men watched me carefully, wondering what I'd pull out next. I put my hand on what I hoped was there. "Gum?' I asked them.

"Hey, all right," Mr. Martin said without a stutter.

We unwrapped our gum and put the sticks in our mouths. Their faces looked like what I was thinking.

"This is hard as a rock," Mr. Wabash said.

"Yes, well," I agreed. "It's frozen. If we were in a hot Oklahoma summer that gum would be a gooey mess and would be hard to chew. At least there's some sugar in it."

Mr. Wabash nodded and chewed his hard Juicy Fruit.

"So, uh, M-M-Miss Black Wolf," Mr. Martin started. "How'd you get that n-n-name?"

"My dad."

"No, I m-m-mean Indians have animal names. How c-c-come?" He limped almost as bad as Mr. Wabash and I figured he may have been talking so he could forget that his knee hurt.

"Not too many Chahtas have animal names. Lots of the animal names you hear are from Indians who've had their traditional names translated. See, Black Wolf in Chahta is *Nashoba Lusa*. Wolf is *lusa* and *nashoba* is black."

"But that would be Wolf Black in English," Jody Jr. said.

"Yes and no. In Chahta, or Choctaw, the noun goes first. Wolf being the noun. The words that modify the noun go after it."

The men nodded their heads as if they knew all about diagramming sentences. Most people hate to do that in English classes. But since I'm trying to learn to speak Choctaw better I have to pay attention to how sentences are put together.

"Lots of Indians changed their names," I lectured. "Or we

know them only by their English versions. Like Crazy Horse, Sitting Bull, Red Cloud. You've heard of them, right?"

They nodded vigorously. If you ask white people to name some Indians they usually come up with these. Of course, a lot of people also list Geronimo. His name was actually Goyanthlay, but that wouldn't make much sense to the men so I didn't mention him.

"Well, we may know them by those names, but they went by their traditional tribal names. And, some Indians didn't translate their names. Many Hopis have long names that are hard to pronounce. But those names have meanings. We don't know what they mean because we don't speak Hopi."

"I can understand th-th-that," Mr. Martin was still thinking. "Lots of immigrants from Europe shortened their n-n-names. Some ch-ch-changed them to sound more American."

I nodded. I knew that already. "Some Indians did that, too. It makes life easier to have a name that people can pronounce." I spoke faster because his stuttering was starting to affect me. "But a lot of Indians who were forced to boarding schools in the 1880s had their names changed by school officials. Indians who went to missionary schools were forced to change their names, too. That's why so many had religious names like John, Paul, Rebecca and Mary after they left school."

"African slaves also had their names changed," offered Mr. Big Jody Johnston.

This is always a depressing subject, but it's also fascinating. Most people don't think about the power of a name. Or the loss of power if it's changed.

"Names are political," I said. I stopped and looked behind me to make certain everyone was in line. "For example, 'Indians' is not what a lot of Indians want to be called."

"What do you want to be called?" asked J.J. Jr.

"My mom prefers indigenous."

"But that's like a plant or animal," said Mr. Martin. "Indigenous means something that was created in a certain place. Like uh," he thought for minute, "you know, bison are indigenous to the United States. So are armadillos and rattlesnakes."

"That's my point. Anthropologists argue that Indians came across the Siberian Land Bridge during an ice age. According to them, that means we came from Europe and slowly migrated throughout the western hemisphere."

"That's right," Mr. Wabash said as he panted. "I learned that all through school."

"Problem is," and I had to keep my cool because I get really touchy about this topic, "there isn't any proof of that."

Now, before you think I'm really well-read about this, I have to tell you I'm not. I listen to Mom and Dad talk about this subject a lot and they know how to respond to those people who believe Indians have no knowledge of anything besides plants and animals.

"There isn't?" asked Mr. Martin.

"Nope." I sighed. "I was raised listening to my creation stories. Those stories say Chahtas were created here, in the Western Hemisphere. Most tribes have stories that tell of their creation here, too. Some were created underground and emerged to the surface, others were created on the surface and moved around here, but they didn't come from Europe."

Before anyone could respond to that tidbit, we arrived at small hill that hid the hunters' camp site that I'd visited already that morning. We'd walked for two hours. If Mr. Wabash had not been injured we could have made it in one hour or less.

He leaned heavily on his tree branch staff and every now and then he'd curse and groan. Mr. Martin stopped and reached down to rub his knee at every opportunity, but he didn't grunt or anything. I was willing to bet that he wouldn't say a word about his knee unless I asked him.

Mr. Wabash had been determined to hike out of his lost situation, regardless of how his friends felt about it and now he was going to pay the price. After numerous sprains, strains and breaks, I knew what the pain felt like and I also knew that he'd feel the pain more after he sat down and rested. Mr. Martin was going to feel pretty bad himself.

As we hiked the hill I told them what the camp looked like and described equipment the hunters had.

"Man, it'll feel g-g-good to sit in a truck," said Mr. Martin.

"Maybe they'll let us have a sandwich," said Big Jody.

"I need some drugs for my foot," moaned Mr. Wabash.

I laughed. "And what do you want, Jody Jr.?"

"A hot bath."

"Good for you." At least the kid knows when he smells.

I reached the crest of the small hill first and when I looked down, my stomach turned.

The hunters had packed up and left. The camp was deserted.

Chapter 9: Camping Should be Fun

After two hours of walking I should have felt warm and sweaty. Instead, a chill snaked up my spine and made me shiver. So far I had dealt with the cold weather, but I had no idea if I could survive a freezing storm that included snow or wet sleet. I was starting to feel more afraid than I ever had.

"We have to stop," I said in a loud voice. "It'll be dark in a few hours and snow's coming." The cold wind swept through the forest as if in agreement with me. I detected snow on the air as sure as I smelled the men's body odor and Jody Baby's feet. "We need to dig in for the night and eat something."

"We can still get out of here," Mr. Wabash argued. His face looked red and he breathed hard.

"No, she's r-r-right," Mr. Martin said. "It's already f-f-four o-clock and we're not gonna get found tonight. Cl-cl-clouds are moving in and we may as well sit still until morning."

"But we have to get home," Mr. Wabash said in a strange high-pitched voice. He sounded scared "It's still early. We can walk some more."

"Walk to where?" I asked yet again. "We're miles away from where we started. You wanted to walk, so we walked. Now we have to stop. Jody needs rest and your ankle's not getting any better." In fact, he was limping worse.

I had other things to worry about. Like where would we make a camp? What would we eat? How do we get a fire started with wet wood? How could I possibly do all these things?

Mom told me once that the best thing to do in case I got lost was to stay calm. Take deep breaths and don't panic, cry or scream.

"People look to each other for strength, Tuli," Mom told me one night after a search had ended badly. I had cried when she told me that she found the bodies of six boy scouts in the cold forests of Arkansas. They had panicked. The scouts died after wandering around for hours in the freezing drizzle. The one survivor said that the pack leader who was an older boy refused to stop and make a fire or to make shelter. He was determined to lead them all back to their base camp.

"That leader realized they were hopelessly lost," Mom told me as she tended to the dogs. It had been a difficult search. "Then he started yelling at the others, telling them it was their fault they were lost. Then he cried. All the time the group was looking to him for guidance."

"But Mom, why didn't he stop and make a camp? All boy scouts know that." Or at least I thought they did.

"Sweetie, when people panic, they don't always think straight. And when people are scared they need someone to tell them what to do." Then Mom looked directly at me and paused so I'd look into her eyes. "Don't you ever forget that if you get lost, do not panic. Do you understand me, Tuli? You have to stay calm and consider the things you've learned."

I looked at the lost hunters and took a deep breath as I thought about her last words that day: "You can survive, Tuli. You may be a girl and some people may think you can't deal with a serious situation, but you know what to do. You have that knowledge in your head."

Jody's father, Jody, brought me back to my situation. "Where did the hunters go?" he asked.

"Maybe they got my note and probably decided to come find me," I answered. "Maybe they drove back to Jacob's Lake. By dirt road it wouldn't take them very long."

Mr. Martin zipped his coat up to his chin. "C-c-cold," he said.

"And it'll get worse," I said. "We have to dig in. And we need to eat."

"I'm not hungry." Mr. Wabash sounded like my brother Pete when he pouts. When Pete wants attention he says he not hungry when he's really starving.

"You haven't had anything t-t-to eat or drink all day, St-St-Stan," said Mr. Martin.

"You're upset, Mr. Wabash." I made it a statement and was prepared to argue with him.

"She's right, Stan," said Jody Sr. He dropped his pack and sat on a log.

I tried to remain clam but felt my nerves jumping. We needed to dig in and we needed to hurry up and get Mr. Wabash and Little Jody warm. "Let's stop and make camp," I said.

"Here?" Mr. Johnston asked with relief in his voice.

"Yes." I took off my pack and reached around behind my waist and unlatched my fanny pack. I put both on the ground and took my folded shovel off the back of the pack.

I pushed aside the pine needle cover and tested the ground. I easily dug into the dirt about six inches. "This'll work," I said.

"My ankle's killing me," said Mr. Wabash. He sat on a log and took off his boot and sock. That was not the right thing to do.

I walked over to inspect his injury. On the outside of the ankle was an enormous purple lump. Now that he had taken off the restricting boot, the swelling increased before my eyes. His entire foot bloated like a balloon slowly inflating.

"I think I broke it."

"Breaks don't usually swell like that. You probably sprained it. Pulled your ligaments."

"I thought it was my tendons."

"No, ligaments hold bones together. When you sprain an ankle the ligaments pull or tear. Tendons attach muscle to bone. You know, like your Achilles tendon. That's the tough one that connects your calf muscle to your heel."

"Geez, it burns," Mr. Wabash said. He took deep breaths to try and keep the pain away.

"I don't doubt it," I said.

"And how would you know?" he asked.

"I've been running for four years. I've turned both my ankles a few times." *But never this bad*, I thought. I was afraid he may have dislocated the bones, but then he wouldn't be walking at all.

"Now that you've t-t-taken off your boot, you're not going to g-g-get it back on for a while," said Mr. Martin.

I nodded in agreement. "I can wrap it, but you have to sit still."

The roll of white medical tape I carried in my pack was old and the goop that made it stick had oozed in the heat of summer and hardened in the cold weather. The tape would have to do. I left his sock on as a first layer so the tape wouldn't rip his skin. Then I alternated sticking twelve inch strips in a U shape under his foot up his leg like straps and then continued with a series of U shapes going from the back of his heel then forward over his arch. I continued to wrap his smelly foot the way Mom taught me until his foot was covered in white.

Then I topped the tape with the ace bandage in my pack, making a sort of figure eight starting around the bottom of his foot and wrapping upwards. That stabilized his ankle, although he could easily turn it again.

"I can't move my foot," he complained.

"That's the idea. That's the same way trainers wrap basketball players' ankles. You'll have to keep your laces loose to get your foot in your boot."

"Neat," Young Jody exclaimed.

"You ever take first aid?" I asked him.

He shook his head.

"You can, you know. At your local YMCA. You never know when you'll have an injury. If you like being outside then you should learn how to deal with problems. If my mom were here she'd stitch your lip."

He took in breath. "She can do that?"

"Yup. Lips heal fast, but you need a few stitches to help it along."

I turned back to digging as the Jodys and Mr. Martin started moving rocks and digging with sticks. It wasn't long before all of us were out of breath.

"Man, the wind sure is coming through here," Big Jody said.

I stood up straight and looked around me. I felt a stab of fear when I realized what I had done. I'd started camp in the worse possible place: in the middle of a small valley open on the southwest and northeast sides. The wind whipped through like cars in the Indy 500. Almost as bad was the reality that if it rained again, we'd be hit with a flood.

What was wrong with me? How could I be so stupid? I watched Mr. Martin as he grunted to move a large rock. The wind blew off his hat and he had to chase it. He came back with his hat and began digging with his gloved hands.

"Stop," I said.

"What?" Asked Mr. Johnston.

"How c-c-come?" Asked Mr. Martin.

"This is a bad spot. We can't stay here."

"What do you mean?" Little Jody asked. He had tried so hard to move rocks that he split his lip again. I got a Kleenex from my back pocket and told him to hold it tightly to his lip.

"My mistake. This is not a good place. We're too vulnerable to the wind and rain."

Mr. Martin cursed.

"Make up your mind," Mr. Johnson added.

"Rest a minute," I said. I walked away from the group and nearly slapped myself for not thinking things through. One of the most basic rules of surviving outdoors is to find adequate shelter.

I was starting to feel humiliated, the same feeling I had after losing the *kapucha* game.

Then I heard my mother's voice again: "Tuli, not thinking means you'll do something stupid."

Okay then. I'd think. Where is the best place to stay the night? I looked around me and considered the trees, the ground cover, the hills around us. To the north was an open field in a valley where Mr. Martin and Johnstons sat resting. No trees or shelter there. The west was rocky. Boulders and rocks of various sizes lay so tightly together there was no place to walk easily, much less to sleep. To the east was a hill, where we'd get hit by winds all night.

Then it hit me all at once: With trees set close enough to block the wind, low branches that would shelter us from heavy snow, and southern exposure, the site already used by the hunters is the perfect spot? How much dumber could I be not to realize that in the first place?

"What's wrong?" Mr. Wabash asked. He sat in his sleeping bag and his voice quivered with cold.

"I picked the wrong place," I told him.

"So pick the right one," he answered. I appreciated that he didn't make a big deal about it. On the other hand, he wasn't in any position to get mad at me. I mean, look what he got himself into.

"I did. We'll stay here," I yelled to the others. I waited until they came over. "There're enough leaves and needles to make the sleeping areas soft and we'll be sheltered."

Mr. Martin came over first. "You sure?" He asked.

"Yes, I'm sure this time." Geez I felt stupid. My face felt hot and I knew I looked embarrassed.

"All right, he answered. He reminded me of my parents who knew I made a big mistake and was willing to overlook it.

"I need to dig a pit so we can cook some food," I said. "You sit down. You just got your knee replaced."

"What? How d-d-did you know that?"

"Someone mentioned it back at Operations. Now sit."

Considering that I almost made a mistake that might cost us very dearly, I felt good saying that. Now they could wonder what else I knew about them. Which wasn't much.

"The Johnstons can clear out the fire pit the other people had. They put dirt all over it but the rock circle's still there. Then find kindling. You know what that is, right?"

"Gee, kid," Mr. Wabash said. "Who doesn't know what kindling is?"

"Just asking."

What I really wanted to say was, since you seem to have no knowledge of being outdoors it makes sense that you wouldn't know about kindling. Mom would really be mad at me if I talked that way to an adult. Even if he deserved it.

I dug a while then Mr. Johnston, Sr. took over, and after a while Mr. Martin limped over and said he wanted to dig. After thirty minutes we had a pretty good sized hole.

"How m-m-much more?" Mr. Martin asked.

"This looks pretty good."

"Now what?" Son of Jody asked. It came out more like "Now hat?" because his lip was so huge.

"We find rocks to put in the bottom. The kind that won't explode when they get hot."

"Like what?" Again, he had trouble with the 'w.' "I mean, what do I look for?" His lip bled after that effort and he put a Kleenex to his mouth.

"Well, we're not near a stream, so pretty much any of these rocks around here are okay. Flat stream and river rocks tend to blow up when they get hot."

We searched around and found a few that would work.

"We need to take those rocks and put them in the bottom of the pit. Then get some sticks and crisscross them on top. Get a fire going in the hole so it's real hot. Then we'll have some good embers to heat the rocks."

"I can do th-th-that," said Mr. Martin.

"You got matches?" I asked him.

"I do."

I watched while he worked at it. Jody II squatted down and watched me unpack. "What you got in there?" He mumbled.

"Let's see. Foil." I handed him the folded squares of aluminum foil. "Carrots." I set out the five big orange vegetables. "Dried onion." Out came the baggy of onion flakes. "Three potatoes."

Mom says she'd rather carry the food in her stomach than on her back. After hauling the big potatoes around all day that made perfect sense to me. Dried potato flakes are handier when carrying your food.

I looked at the fire project. The flames had kicked up for about twenty minutes, then they died and the embers glowed.

"And the best of all. Half a roast." I pulled it out and set it inside the small cook pot.

Mr. Wabash let out a yelp. I thought he was laughing, but looking closer I saw that he was crying. He had his hand over his face and cried softly.

I averted my eyes to my pack. He felt afraid and probably foolish. Actually, I felt pretty much the same. His ankle probably hurt, too. I hardly ever see men cry and wasn't sure what to say. I don't like to see anyone upset.

"And, almost the best." I took out another baggie.

"What's that?" Asked Papa Jody.

"I collect spice packets from fast food places. You know, salt, pepper, sugar, mustard and ketchup packs. And soy sauce."

"I never th-th-thought of that," said Mr. Martin.

"A little spice can make a lot of difference. Take a piece of foil and a slice of meat. Then take a carrot, some onion and potato slices. Sprinkle some of the spices on it then fold up the foil and we'll put it in the pit and cover it up."

I took out one of my three knives and handed it to Mr. Martin. Next, I got out my camp kit silverware, that being a fork and large spoon.

"I've never done this before," said the Jodys simultaneously.

"You can cook all kinds of stuff underground. Some people cook whole pigs, sheep, whatever. Vegetables make it taste better. Normally, if you have just a few items you'd put everything in a pot and bury it, but my pot's too small."

"What d-d-do I do now?" Mr. Martin yelled from the fire pit.

"Take the shovel and move the embers to the side, off the rocks. We'll lay the foil packs on the racks. Then we'll cover them with embers and dirt for about an hour."

"Interesting," he exclaimed. Then he nodded and tried to kneel down to move the embers. His right leg didn't want to bend.

I got up and went over to him. "I'll do it. Go sit down with your leg straight."

"Th-th-thanks." He said it quietly. Mr. Martin looked to be the kind of person who wanted to help at every opportunity and he was embarrassed when he couldn't.

For the next hour the food cooked while I did my best to direct the uninjured men in making a comfortable camp for the night. We used my little shovel, branches and our hands to dig out a deep, wide hole in the ground. After a while we had a hole about seven feet by seven feet by two feet deep.

"I'll g-g-get more wood," said Mr. Martin. Little wood pieces lay everywhere and kindling was easy to find. I like it when people volunteer to work, but with his recent knee surgery he didn't need to be running around.

Little Jody stepped up to the plate. "I'll do it."

I looked at him and gave him a thumb's up which reminded me of my brother Pete. He sure didn't feel like hunting for wood, either.

The wind increased, forcing more cold down my collar. "*Mali ut hlampko micha kapassa*," I said aloud.

"Say what?' Mr. Martin asked.

"The wind's strong and cold. Snow's on the way."

"Oh."

"Hey, look at where we were going to camp," Little Jody yelled to us.

We looked to where he pointed, to the spot where we had been preparing for the night. The wind swirled so furiously that sticks and dirt spiraled upwards.

"Dirt devil," I said in a quiet voice. We could have been right in the middle of it. My face felt hot again.

I took out one of the tarps in my pack and lay it on the ground, then folded it in half so we could sit on it. After we got in for the night, I'd lay the other tarps on top of us to keep the snow off.

I uncovered dirt on the cooking pit. Using two long sticks I removed the hot foil packs. I unfolded one and poked at the meat with the tip of my knife. "Looks ready," I said.

Each of us took a foil pack and sat on the tarp. My pack had ripped a bit and my carrot was burned. It looked pretty terrible. Most people would cringe at the thought of eating a pile of food with ashes on top of it.

But things change when you're outdoors. Crispy pieces and even bits of dirt and tree bark taste pretty good when you're hungry. Mom says it's all a part of man's natural instincts. "When you're feeling empty, you'll eat whatever it takes to fill you up," she told me. "That's why starving people eat insects and raw food they wouldn't normally touch if McDonalds is nearby."

People get grossed out watching "Fear Factor," but Mom never flinches.

And if you're scared and thinking that you might die of starvation, well, food cooked underground like this is better than any candy or ice cream. I couldn't help but wonder once again at how my ancestors managed to survive without modern utensils and pizza. They did manage very well, though, and the least I could do is to honor them by not complaining about all my modern conveniences like tin foil, Goretex and Bic lighters.

I watched as the men ate every bite of their dinners. Jody and Jody ate very fast while Mr. Wabash looked at each morsel before he put it in his mouth. Mr. Martin appeared to be by far the largest of the three men, but he ate very slowly. He looked afraid to finish because then there'd be no more food.

"That was just gr-gr-great," said Mr. Martin. "Really. Just great." He neatly folded the foil and handed it to me. He brushed some food out of his big moustache.

"What are gonna do for breakfast?" Asked Mr. Worry Wart. I mean Mr. Wabash.

"We need to look in everyone's pack and see what we have," I said, although with his weight he could live off his fat a while.

My pack lay at my feet and I pulled it close to me and rooted around in it. "I have a bag of dried apricots, a hunk of cheddar cheese, a bag of dried milk, macaroni, dehydrated spaghetti sauce, dried peppers, a pack of smoked salmon, three cans of Beenie Weenies, two cans of corn, two rolls of *banaha*, and a granola bar that's all squashed. Plus this roll of butterscotch Lifesavers." I put the items back in the pack. "And a roll of dental floss in my coat pocket. Need some?"

"What the heck's *banaha*?"

"It's cornmeal and bean dough placed in corn shucks, tied with strips of shuck, then cooked under hot ashes. Mom likes it the old way with hickory oil, but I like it with garlic and soy sauce. In the old days *banaha* could be stored for months and re-cooked. We can have this in the morning. I'll heat it up."

"Cool," Jody Jr. remarked.

Mr. Wabash shook his head. His teeth appeared to be distinctly yellow and I doubted that he flossed much.

"That's not a lot," noticed Mr. Wabash. "I thought you were a rescue person."

I gritted my nice clean teeth to remind myself to be polite. Then I answered him. "Most search and rescue personnel don't expect to stay out all night like this. Normally they go out and back to the operations site several times a day."

Jody Junior had difficulty keeping food in his mouth as he chewed and I got distracted by the dinner that dropped to his lap.

I continued. "I grabbed a few items from my mom's stash of food in case I got caught out here. Normally I'd never bring a roast since it takes a long time to cook. Besides, I'm not a real search and rescue person. I'm learning. In winter you should bring cheese and butter."

Everyone was silent a few seconds.

"You're doing fine," said Jody, Sr.

That comment made me think about my mistake in almost putting us in the wrong camping spot.

"My head hurts," said Mr. Wabash. He rubbed his left temple for effect.

I reached into my fanny pack and took out a pack of Motrin then tossed it to him. The square pack landed on his big leg and fell off into the dirt where it had to search for it.

"What else you got in there?" Son Jody mumbled through his sore lip. I tried hard to be courteous and not look at it, but there was his lip in front of me like a big, swollen, purple tick.

"The fanny pack's where I keep all the stuff I need for basic survival. Knife, matches, extra gloves, hat, socks. I also have sunscreen, lip balm, Neosporin, Dr. Scholl's pads for blisters. Other first aid things. Candy bar that I ate already. A lot of other things that are stuck into the pockets. Quarters. A twenty dollar bill. Note pad and pencil."

I poked my larger pack with my foot. "In that bigger pack I got much of the same stuff, but more clothes, a tarp, toilet paper, plastic bags, matches, a light rope, sewing kit, fish hooks, string, small hacksaw, extra sunglasses, mirror, diapers, a big wool sweater and dead batteries for my radio."

"Dead batteries?" asked Mr. Wabash.

"Yeah. I change out my batteries each season and forgot to last spring. They're dead. If I was a real rescue person that would never happen."

I was thinking that Mom would have a fit once she found out I didn't change the batteries. I mean, look at what happened because I goofed up. My face burned once more but it was too late to get mad at myself. All I could do now was to learn from my errors.

"Diapers?" asked Jody Jr.

"Yeah," I answered. People tend to think it's funny to carry around diapers. "For bad cuts. Diapers are made to be absorbent."

I reached into the bottom of my pack and was surprised at what I pulled out next: a small roll of orange material inside a box.

"What's that?" asked Mr. Martin.

I tossed him the box and he looked at the label. "Emergency survival bag," he said. "It's made of a m-m-micro-thin layer of aluminized f-f-film laminated to a c-c-composite reinforced ripstop m-m-material. Does it work?"

"Oh yes," I answered. "Even in water." How could I have forgotten about this bag? I could have used it the night before and been perfectly warm, as warm as I was after piling all kinds of tarps and needles on top of me. "I think Mr. Wabash should sleep in that. The bag keeps in the heat and he needs the most help right now."

"I agree," said Mr. Johnston. Mr. Martin took the material out of the box and slowly unrolled it until it became a six-foot orange bag. He helped Mr. Wabash slide into it, then zipped the side and pulled the end over his head, like a hat.

No one else had an emergency bag, or even a sleeping bag. We'd have to make do under the two tarps. Well, if I did it the night before I could do it again this night.

Smoke from the fire wafted across our faces and we flinched. I looked up to see dark clouds obscuring the stars. A few clouds allowed us to see the full and bright moon. If the clouds had been soft and fluffy, the moon light would have shone though them. These clouds were black and angry. The wind grew fiercer.

"Okay, give me your foil," I told the others. "We may have to use it again."

I folded the foil and put it inside a baggie.

"Now what?" Asked Mr. Martin.

"We need to get into our hole. But before we do that, we have to cover that fire pit with big pieces of wood so the snow won't fill it up. Then we need to find wood and stack it around the edge of our hole so we can get it easily. We're gonna have some weather and after snow comes it'll be hard finding wood under a foot of white stuff."

Mr. Wabash grimaced as he started to stand.

"Not you," I told him. "You need to sit still."

He started to argue with me and thought better of it. Severe pain does that. As he situated himself, I noticed that he didn't wear a wool sweater under his coat.

"What layers do you have on under that jacket?" I asked him.

"Uh. T-shirt, a long sleeved t-shirt, and a sweater my wife got me."

I walked over and reached to his neck. "Can I see that material?"

"Yeah, sure."

"It's not wool," I said.

"I know," he answered.

"It feels like heavy cotton, like a sweatshirt."

"I think it's Hanes brand."

"You need a wool sweater. You have one in your bag?"

"Nope. Just another sweater like this one. It's red."

"It has no insulation power. You can freeze to death. Let me see what size my extra sweater is."

I pulled it from my pack and looked at the label. "It's a large. I got it from my dad because it was too small for him. Take off everything except that first t-shirt and put this on. It'll be small on you, but it'll keep you warm."

"I don't need that, kid," he said.

"Yes, you do."

"Come on St-St-Stan. Put it on," said Mr. Martin as he bent down and began unzipping Stan's jacket. "I'll help you out of th-th-this."

As Mr. Martin dealt with Mr. Wabash the rest of us fanned out, collected fuel, then returned to our spot with armfuls of wood. Most of it was dry aspen and pine branches.

"You know," said Father Jody, "we better get more wood because aspen and pine burns fast."

"All wood burns fast," said Mr. Wabash.

"We don't burn much wood in Oklahoma," I said, "but I know that the best kind to have at night is oak because it's thick, heavy and it burns slow. You don't have to wake up to tend the fire."

I went back into the forest to find more wood. I took a deep breath of clean, high desert air. I knew that under normal circumstances I'd be enjoying myself on a cold, but nice camping trip.

"Now we have to cover that pit," I reminded the weary hunters. "Find some logs to criss-cross over the hole. On top of that we need to put some branches with needles still on it."

"I'm beat," said Mr. Martin. He stopped and put his hands on his hips and bent over, like runners do when they're out of breath.

I didn't say anything and he noticed. Evidently the silence embarrassed him because he started moving. After we scurried around to find the necessary wood, I stuck a long branch into the ground next to the pit. No telling what kind of snow we'd be getting that night, and I didn't want to dig through it in the morning to find another fire place. The tall stick would hopefully mark the spot.

I walked a few steps then stopped as I thought better of my idea.

"We have to protect that fire better," I said.

"And how do we do that?" asked Mr. Wabash.

"We need some long branches with brush on the ends. Put the branches upright so they touch in the middle. We can use some of my rope and tie the tops together. That'll keep snow from falling on the pit and we won't have so much to bail out in the morning."

The men held the branches while I tied the four pieces together with nice cow hitches then I secured the last branch with a basic square knot.

"What kind of knot is that?" Jody Jr. asked.

I told him. "Unless the rope gets wet and freezes, it should be easy to untie in the morning. You should get your dad to buy you a survival book. Use some light rope and practice."

"Hey, Dad . . ."

"I heard. I will."

We went back to our hole in the ground. Mr. Wabash sat with his legs out in front of him and a hand over his face. He hurt.

"Here are two more trash bags," I said. "Let's cover as much of that wood as we can. And put some of it in the hole with us. We can use the small pieces for kindling in the morning."

"But its uncomfortable sitting on this stuff," said Mr. Wabash.

"You don't have to sit on it, but if we don't think about keeping it dry tonight, tomorrow we're gonna be sorry that we didn't save some wood."

"Yeah, yeah. Okay, okay."

We got our wood stash ready for the night and we got into our hole. I leaned back and felt that the top of the edge of the hole was only to my shoulder blades. That meant that it was only up to the men's lower backs and the wind would bother them.

"We need to dig in deeper," I told them.

"I'm too tired," said Mr. Wabash.

"If we don't get deeper into the ground the snow will pile up and we'll get covered and wet. We need to get in here another foot. I'll start then we'll take turns."

"Good idea," said Mr. Martin.

We dug and removed rocks and other debris for an hour. As I worked I thought about the winter survival seminar I attended with Mom. "A survival expert told our group one time that when you're trying to survive outdoors, 'if you lose your gloves you lose your life.'" I said aloud to the group. "So, be careful not to rip your gloves. Mom tells us stuff like that to make her points. Quotes like that scare me. And that's the point. I never forget them."

"What?" Mr. Wabash looked surprised that I said that.

"Well, it's true. If you're out in the cold and you don't have gloves, your hands can freeze. The more you rub the more you ruin the tissue. Most people rub frostbitten hands together to get them warm, but the friction tears the tender tissue that's been frozen. If you pour warm water over your hands you may feel warm for a minute, but the water on your hands freezes and you start the problem all over again."

"I didn't know that," Jody the Lip said.

I kept digging and realized that the men were quiet. I looked up and all four had their hands in their pockets.

"Look," I said," it's not snowing yet and y'all have extra gloves, right?"

No one answered.

"Right?"

"I d-d-don't," answered Mr. Martin. "These are it."

"Same here," said Mr. Wabash.

"We have mittens in the pack," Large Jody said quietly. All the men looked embarrassed.   Well, it's not like I never make a mistake. "You should always have an extra pair of gloves," I said. "You need liner gloves, then warm, waterproof gloves and another pair of waterproof mittens for night or for a cold, windy day to wear over your gloves."

They didn't reply to that and I kept digging. My back ached and my leg throbbed. I would have dug into the hole more if my little shovel hadn't finally broken off at the neck.

"We're done with this," I said. "Okay, everybody can get in." The men situated themselves in the hole and after a few minutes of squirming around they settled into their nest.

After they became still I asked, "What's in your packs?"

Jody the Dad shrugged. "Extra clothes mainly. Game bag in case we killed something. Extra ammo."

"S-s-same here," added Mr. Martin.

I looked at Mr. Wabash. "I brought my camera, film and a Frisbee," he said. "A sweater and plastic bags. We all have our rifles."

A frisbee?

I looked at Little Jody. "Mom gave me a baggy with vitamins."

"Good idea," I said, trying to be nice. I mean, vitamins don't have calories, which is what we needed at the moment.

Okay. So here we have it. These men went hunting in a densely wooded, sparsely populated area that featured only a few roads and no place to take shelter in case they got in trouble. Bad weather was coming and none of these guys brought radios, batteries, emergency tent, or first aid items. The feeling of fear gnawed at me again.

"Anyone bring any food? Any at all?"

Mr. Wabash and Mr. Martin shook their heads no. Jody Sr. sighed and said he had four bags of peppered beef jerky. I grit my teeth. The problem with store-bought jerky is that it's heavily salted which means you need to drink a lot of water if you plan on eating it.

"No snacks except for jerky?"

They shook their heads.

"Any water?"

They all nodded and smiled. "I got two bottles," said Son Jody.

"And I got a gallon jug in here," said Mr. Wabash.

"I brought a P-P-Pepsi," said Mr. Martin. "I drank it already but I got the bottle."

Not enough water, either. I tried not to yell out of frustration. Instead I closed my eyes, felt the first cold, wet snow flakes hit my face, then considered what to do next.

Chapter 10: A Very Cold Night

"It's getting cold," observed Mr. Wabash.

The heavy snow fell steadily now. Wet snow is cold snow.

I sat without moving. I knew I needed to get up and find more wood. I needed to make certain that Mr. Wabash's foot was warm. I had to check the fire pit to see if it was protected from snow.

Now I knew how Mom felt. She'd make dinner, clean dishes, then make sure that Pete and I were bathed and had brushed our teeth. This was after she helped us with homework and school projects. Then she'd go from room-to-room to pick up dirty clothes and dishes. She'd wipe down the counters, make our school lunches and then clean the potties.

Well, I sure had a new respect for all the things my Mom did for our family. Was I supposed to get mad at these men for not behaving like they should behave as hunters? Or, was I supposed to be gentle and educate them? I felt like Mom now. No wonder she gets headaches.

I took the garbage bags from the outside pocket of my pack and told Mr. Wabash to get out his bags.

"Look," I said to the other three. "Take these bags and make a hole for your head. Slide it on. It helps keep in body heat. You could do it for your bottom, but since we aren't little we can't get our legs in here. So, sit on the bags in case your body melts the snow under you."

Mr. Wabash still wore his cowboy hat. "That's a nice hat," I told him. "But you need to take it off and put on a wool cap."

"What for?"

"That cowboy hat won't keep the heat in. You got another hat?"

"Yeah, a black one."

"Use it then pull that bag up over that."

"I brought a t-t-tarp," said Mr. Martin. Snow had already collected in his moustache and I knew it would freeze overnight.

"Well, get it out, dummy," scolded Mr. Wabash.

"Spread it over you and the Jodys to keep the snow off you," I said. "It'll melt right into your clothes. Plus it'll keep all of you warmer."

"Why don't we make a bigger fire in the middle here?" Asked the Big Johnston. His jaw quivered from the cold.

"It would be too easy to get burned. It can catch our tarps on fire. And if it snows then we can't keep the fire covered and burning. I mean, we could if we had an igloo. But I don't know how to make a good one. I think I could make a snow cave, though."

For a few seconds the snow fell so hard and fast we couldn't see each other from across the pit. The air smelled clean and alive.

"Looks like you may get a chance," Mr. Wabash said. He sounded tired and weak.

"You okay?" I asked him.

"Just pooped."

Something about head injuries tugged at my brain, but I couldn't see it clearly. "You smoke?" I asked.

"Yeah. Not today though."

"Mr. Johnston, take his pulse. At his wrist."

The two men looked at each other. Mr. Wabash started to object while Mr. Johnston looked sheepish. "Come on," Big Jody said. "Let me try."

Mr. Wabash pulled back his sleeve and took off his glove. Mr. Johnston felt around for a pulse and finally said, "I feel it. Thready. You look kinda pale."

"I'm a red head. I am pale."

"No, I mean paler."

"It's hard to get a deep breath," Mr. Wabash replied.

Oh no, I thought, but didn't say out loud. He did look different with out the cowboy hat. Somehow the cap made him look smaller.

"If you need to go, then do it now," I said instead.

"Go? Go where?" Asked Mr. Martin.

"You know. The bathroom."

"Oh, right," Mr. Wabash said weakly, yet sarcastically. "Those nice warm bathrooms behind the trees over there."

"Suit yourself," I answered. "But if you have to go in the middle of the night then you may get covered in snow that'll melt and you'll get even colder. And if it snows hard you may get lost."

"She's got a p-p-point," Mr. Martin said. "I'm going."

"Us too," added the Jodys.

After relieving myself in the darkness of the woods, I buried my little bit of toilet paper then returned to the hole where we all settled back into our spots. You're supposed to pack out everything you take in, that includes t.p. However, I wasn't in the mood to mind proper camping etiquette.

I pulled my knit hat down on my forehead. Then I lifted my coat collar to completely cover my neck. I pulled one of the trash bags over my head and pulled the tie around my waist. The snow fell harder and a strand of hair caught in my spider earring.

I made certain that the tarp covered my body up to my neck and that it sheltered Mr. Wabash. I looked across the fire to the Jodys. "Y'all covered up over there?" I asked.

"Yeah," answered the Little One. "I guess."

"Tuck the ends under your legs. It's gonna snow a lot and if it does we'll be covered by morning. You have to keep as dry as you can. Don't keep your legs curled under you."

"But I'm cold," Mr. Wabash yelled weakly over the wind.

I leaned towards him and put my hand on his foot, or at least on the lump that I thought was his foot. When Dad tells me stories he sits on the end of my bed and puts one hand on my foot. He sits at the end of the bed instead of next to me because Pete always comes in my room for story time and lays sideways over my legs while Dad talks. Dad telling stories makes me feel safe and warm. Maybe a story would work for Mr. Wabash.

"You know," I began, "one time long ago two Choctaw hunters became lost in the woods. They became cold and very hungry. They only had one little rabbit left to eat. As they watched the spitted rabbit cook over the fire, they heard a woman crying in the woods. They found a lady dressed in white sitting under a tree. They brought her back to their little fire and asked who she was. She told them she was the daughter of Hashtali and Moon Mother, and while she was out doing an errand for them, she ran out of food then became very weak."

I looked at my hand covering his foot and tried not to cry as I finished the story.

"They gave her their rabbit, but she only took one bite. Then she told them they would be rewarded for their kindness. She told them to come back the next morning to where they found her. Then she just disappeared. The hunters were shocked, but still very hungry so they ate what was left of the rabbit."

"The next morning the hunters returned to where they found the lady and in her spot was a green plant over six feet tall. It had a golden tassel at the top. The leaves were long. The hunters took one of the long fruits that grew from between the leaves. He peeled back the green covering and found small seeds set in neat rows. He took a bite and realized that the food would taste better cooked. They took the remaining ears home, cooked and ate them. Then they planted the kernels in the spring. In the fall, they had a crop of the new food they called *tanchi*. This is how corn became the tribe's favorite food."

No one said anything.

"Do you believe that?" Mr. Martin asked me.

"Sure. Why not?"

"Okay," was all he said.

I looked at Mr. Wabash who had a sleepy smile on his face. Maybe my story made him feel better. Or bored him to sleep. Either way, he was quiet.

"Cool," said Jody Jr.

"I think so. Lots of tribes have stories dealing with women who bring food to the tribe. They're symbols of sustenance."

"Sustenance?" he asked.

"Food. The things that keep people alive. Corn is a symbol of sustenance and life. And it's very female."

"Female?"

"Almost every tribe has creation stories that place women in key roles. Female had powerful positions in tribes. In politics, religion, economy, social life."

"What do you mean in politics?" His dad asked.

"Well, in Iroquois tribes, elder women declared and stopped war. They chose the leaders and decided how to punish their enemies if they were caught. They also controlled the crop production and decided what their trade items would be."

"They chose leaders?" Mr. Martin was surprised.

"Oh yes. And a lot more than that. Women and men were equal back then."

"And they are today," Little Jody said.

No one said anything.

"Aren't they?"

"Son," his dad said solemnly, "I'll talk to you about that when we get home."

A huge gust of wind blew across our tarp, hitting our faces with ice crystals that stung like ant bites.

"Dang," yelled the Jodys.

"You have to keep your blood moving," I told them. "Straighten and bend your legs to keep your blood flowing."

The wind died as quickly as it started. I wondered if my mom was out looking for me and if she felt scared for me. She should know that I'd dig in, but in this weather, she couldn't help but worry about my leg and if I could walk.

"My hand's c-c-cut," said Mr. Martin.

"When did you do that?" I asked him.

"Yesterday. In winter m-m-my hands get dry. I let them air dr-dr-dry after I wash them. Then I get spl-spl-splits around my thumb."

"That's common. My heels do that in summer if I don't put on socks after I shower." I reached into my big pack under the tarp and took out my flashlight and a small tube of super glue. "Once I had to get a stitch to close up a split in my heel. Give me your hand," I said.

"It doesn't c-c-come off." He was the only one to laugh at that. Then he stretched towards me so his thumb was under my nose.

"Can't see. Just a sec." I unscrewed the top of my flashlight and took out the batteries. Too bad they didn't fit my walkie talkie.

"What are you doing?" He asked.

"Taking out this little piece of cardboard between the batteries so it won't accidentally turn on in my pack. I learned that from my dad." I put the flashlight back together and pushed the switch button. Luckily, the batteries were still juicy.

I shined it on his thumb. Sure enough, his skin by the nail had split deeply. I put a small squirt of glue on his wound. "Let that dry then put your glove on."

"Neat trick," he said as he inspected his sealed thumb.

"How you doing, Jody Jr.?" I asked.

"I'm okay," he said quietly.

"You warm?"

"I wish it was summer."

119

"Summer's nice," I agreed. "Oklahoma is hot in summer. Most days I have to shower twice because I sweat so much. Rains help the fields, trees and lawns grow like crazy. Tomatoes and squashes grow faster than dandelions. Bugs fly around everywhere. I have to keep brushing those tiny gnats away from my nose and for some reason that only makes more of them bother me."

I took a deep breath and tried to imagine taking in the green, moist Oklahoma air filled with life and history. Instead, cold, damp air rushed into my lungs and I coughed.

"Nice and green, huh?" Asked Mr. Johnston.

I nodded and wiped my nose. "Very green. There're millions of birds who live in the green trees. We have lots of oaks, pecans and cottonwood. Sometimes big grasshoppers jump out of the brush and hit my leg."

The truth really is that I love summer in Oklahoma. Sure, I spend a lot of time running and aching and then sitting on our covered back porch as the days heated up. The bags of frozen peas I use as ice packs thawed quickly on my warm, but aching knee and thigh.

On one of those days a mosquito landed on my shin and I watched her as she prepared to drink my blood. Only female mosquitoes drink blood, you know. And her proboscis is so sharp and thin you usually don't even feel it going in. It itches like crazy later, though. When she was about to poke me I knocked her off me with a good flick from my middle finger.

As I sat in the freezing weather I recalled when Happy sat on my feet while John ran around the backyard after yellow and white butterflies as they flitted about our flower garden. John caught them easily. After all, they don't fly very fast. After getting one in her mouth she realized they tasted bad so she decided to just chase them.

Then Mom came home from her run all sweaty. She came around to the backyard where she took off her shoes before holding the hose on the top of her head. I know that when Mom's tired and has salty sweat in her eyes after a run she doesn't like to talk. So I didn't say anything as I watched her squirt water on her head and legs, then turn off the water and stretch.

"Good run?" I asked as she went inside.

"Pretty good," she answered.

Pete came out to the porch with a jam-smeared graham cracker in his hand.

"Geez. Pete," I said. "How much are you gonna eat?"

"I'm in a growth spurt," he answered.

"A sideways spurt at the rate you're going."

"I timed Mom," Pete said. "She ran faster than you did."

"Gee thanks for telling me that Pete and making me feel good. How do you know she went faster? You don't even know how far she went."

"She told me."

"She did not."

"Did too."

Before we started a full-blown yelling match, Mom came out with a large glass filled with water. She had changed into fresh clothes and a tube of moisturizer stuck out of a back pocket of her shorts.

Mom put a chair cushion on the deck and sat on it. "*Omba chi ahoba*-Storm's coming," she said as she rubbed the lotion on her legs.

I looked up and around at the sky and didn't see anything except fluffy white clouds.

"I feel it in my knees," she said. Mom has had several knee surgeries and her knees throb whenever it's cold or wet weather is about to happen.

Happy trotted over and sat next to Mom. She put her nose to Mom's ear. "Good girl," Mom said as she scratched Happy's chin. "I have to go to the store. We're out of salad stuff. Pete, get dressed and we'll all go."

My brother went in the house to put on a shirt and Mom finished rubbing on lotion. It's so humid in the Oklahoma summer that we really don't need lotion, but Mom's worried about getting wrinkles. She doesn't forget my mistakes, either. Like when I took two dogs instead of the one she told me to take.

"If they saw a coyote or a deer, they'd yank your arm out of joint and drag you."

"I haven't seen a coyote in three weeks."

"I saw two today standing by the side of the road. And I saw a deer last night."

"How come you always see them?"

"Because I keep my eyes open."

We sat in silence a moment. A gray mourning dove cooed from the shelter of pecan tree leaves. Thunder boomed in the distance. Hummingbirds zoomed around the porch in attempts to be the only drinkers at the red sugar-water feeder shaped like a strawberry.

"Okay, let's get to the store. A university student wants to talk about search and rescue and I invited her over for dinner."

I stood to go inside and took my bags of warm peas with me.

"S-s-sounds nice," Said Mr. Martin.

"I thought Oklahoma was desert," said Mr. Wabash.

"Oh, no. It's real green and lush and moist. All kinds of animals there. And there's more shoreline in Oklahoma than in Minnesota."

"Is that a lot?" asked Mr. Johnston.

"Well, you know. Minnesota is the Land O' Lakes."

"Oh, yeah. Like the butter."

I ignored that. Land O' Lakes uses a stereotypical drawing of a Native woman on its label for butter and eggs, at least. Mom won't buy anything with stereotypes on it. "Anyway, it's hot and sweaty summer you'd say you wished it was winter. Move closer to your dad, Jody."

"So, uh," started Mr. Martin. "What were you s-s-saying about Indians being created here in the United St-St-States?" We all knew it might be a long night and needed something to talk about.

"That's what I've been told all my life."

A loud, mournful howl shot through the darkness.

"What was that?" Mr. Wabash asked loudly. "Is that a wolf?"

"Wolves are here?" Mr. Martin looked around.

"*Nashoba holba.* That's a coyote," I said. "They're everywhere."

"Are they gonna come in here and attack us?"

"Hardly. Coyotes sound scary but they have other things to look at besides us. Don't worry. They won't bother us."

"You sure?" asked Mr. Johnston.

"Pretty sure. We have a million coyotes around our house in Oklahoma and they never come around."

"Does your dad hunt?" Asked Mr. Johnston.

"No. He did when he was a kid. But he wounded a duck once and it made him sick. He brought it home and when its wing was healed he let it go. He told me it didn't make sense to heal something that he'd just go hunt again."

"I thought you'd like to hunt," he said. "I mean you like being outside, right?"

"Just because I like being in the woods and tracking animals doesn't mean I want to kill them."

They thought about that one. Lots of hunters hunt because it's a guy thing, a way to bond with other men. Women hunt too, although I don't understand why, unless they're trying to feed their families or to show that they can do anything that men can do. That's Mom's theory, anyway.

"You play sports?" Jody Jr. asked.

"I play *kapucha*."

"What's that?"

"It's our version of lacrosse. Or I should say our sport developed into lacrosse."

"They play it lot back east," his dad said.

"We use sticks we make ourselves out of hickory wood and sinew. We call them *kabocca* and they're about three feet long with pockets at the end. Men players a long time ago stripped to the waist and wore paint on their chests, sometimes with a horse, raccoon or puma tail and put feathers on their heads, arms and waists."

"Did women play?" Big Jody asked.

"Oh yes. After the men played. They were just as aggressive. People got broken arms, legs, faces. Some even died from getting hit so hard. My great grandpa had his knee dislocated in a game and Mom says he had a big scar across his nose from being hit so hard."

"Why do you do it? " Mr. Wabash asked quietly. I guess he wasn't asleep after all.

"It's not as violent as it used to be. I guess I play because it makes me feel like I belong. Like I'm a part of the tribe. A part of the past. Every time I pick up my *kabocca* I feel, I feel . . .," I tried and couldn't find the word. I never had to express what I thought about playing *kapucha* before.

"Like it's right?" Little Jody mumbled.

"Yes. That's it. I feel right."

The wind whistled through the trees and a branch broke off with a pop and fell to the ground with a crash.

"Oh, man," said Mr. Johnston.

"It's a part of nature," I said. "Don't be scared of it." That's the exact thing Jaunty told me one night after a strong wind broke her peach tree in half.

"So," I asked them. "What would you do if you got a deer? Do you know how to dress it?"

"I brought a book," said Mr. Wabash.

"Hmmm," was my Mom-like response.

"Do you know how to dress a deer?" Little Jody asked.

"I know how because I've seen it done. But I've never done it. My father's father was a skilled hunter although he never seemed to have a sharp knife. He spent most of his time sharpening. So whenever he had a deer I watched him. It took quite a while each time."

"Is he still alive?"

"No. He died one morning after a drunken lady hit his Ford head on. My grandpa hadn't had a drink in five years. He wore his seat belt, but he died instantly. The drunk lady got thrown from her car through the passenger window and landed in the alfalfa. She had a broken wrist, a bad hangover and a week in jail. Go figure."

That's a hard story to ask questions about. So they started on another track.

"And so, and so . . . ." Mr. Martin had a hard time finding the words. "What about God?"

"What about God?" I asked. I knew someone was going to bring that up.

"We all c-c-came from Adam and Eve. And they weren't here in t-t-the United States."

"The United States wasn't here when Adam and Eve were alive, Henry," Mr. Wabash said.

Cold, stinging wind ran past us again like darts headed for a dart board.

"Look," I said. "None of us were here at creation, so how do we know what happened?"

"You go to ch-ch-church?" He asked.

"I've been to church."

"You read the B-B-Bible?"

"Of course. It's a great book."

He was silent a few seconds.

"What about being a Chr-Chr-Christian. You a Christian? Your Mom and Dad Christians?"

"Sort of."

"How can you sort of be a Christian?" Mr. Wabash asked.

"Easy. Believe in God. Believe in Jesus. Have a lot of questions."

"But no faith."

"Sure I have faith. I have faith that good will win. I have faith that Hashtali is watching us."

"Who?" Asked Mr. Martin.

"God."

"Okay, okay, you guys," said Jody Sr. "Enough religious talk. No one wins in that. Like taxes. And voting."

"True," I added. I knew that already. I get in a lot of conversations about religion. No one wins especially when the topic of September 11 gets thrown into the mix. But, we can try to educate each other.

"Clear sky," said Jody the Boy.

I looked up to see bright stars through the pine branches. The dark clouds had blown away for the moment, but I knew more would take their place.

"Nothing to dim their light except the moon," I said. "No street lights. No stadium lights. See that set of seven stars right above, it looks like a cross? At the end, the northeast end—more east, really, is a big bright star. That's Cygnus, the swan. Some people call it the northern cross."

A cloud blew across our line of sight and blocked out the stars. Mr. Wabash coughed.

"That's the front line." I said.

"Front line of what?" Mr. Wabash asked.

"The front. Feel that?" The temperature had dropped dramatically in the past few minutes. "Keep your hat on tonight. That keeps body heat in."

"You Indians know your stuff," said Jody Sr.

"What do you mean?" I asked. I figured it had to do with the stereotype about my natural tracking ability, or some other silly belief such as Indians having the eyes of eagles. Boy and Girl Scouts tend to latch on to those images.

"You found us. You know how to make fire and cook outside."

I laughed a good laugh. "Boy, if you only knew how many stereotypes I have to deal with."

They all looked at me.

"Look, let's put it this way. . ."

Before I tell you what I told my new friends, I need to tell you that I've listened to Mom's answer for years. I agree with what she says, although I have my own take about how people view Indians.

". . . it's true I happen to be good at tracking and no, it's not because my Indian genes endow me with the eyes of a hawk with binoculars and the nose of wolf. I had to learn all the skills just like everyone else."

Does this sound rehearsed? It is. I have to talk about search and rescue a lot at my school. Not because I'm so great at it, but because of my famous mother.

I continued. "Hundreds of hours of first aid, radio, map and compass, survival, environmental hazards and tracking training puts all us search and rescue folks on the same playing field. But how you use what you learn is key. That's the hardest part."

"You spend a lot of time doing this, huh?" asked Little Jody. He sounded interested.

"All the time. Mom and Dad talk about animals and tracking every day."

"What does your d-d-dad do?" asked Mr. Martin.

"He's a vet. He specializes in horses, cows, elephants and tigers."

"Cool," exclaimed Jody Jr.

His dad laughed.

"No, really. He tends to elephants and tigers in the zoos around Oklahoma, Texas, Missouri and Kansas. Dad taught us about serious first aid and how to stitch. Mom's first aid kit is as well-stocked as a paramedic's. Of course, she is a paramedic."

"Your mom does searches all the time?" asked Jody Sr.

"She teaches third grade."

"Wow," Little Jody exclaimed. "I bet they like her."

"She has all kinds of show and tells. Animal bones, plaster casts of tracks, our dogs. Last spring she took the class to the woods and showed them how to track. They had to identify three animal tracks and three plants."

"Dang," he answered. "I never get to do stuff like that."

"You can do it by yourself, you know. Go to the library and get tracking books. Read about animals, animal tracks, knots, survival, camping. You can get a lot off the web, too. It's fun. And you won't be afraid when you get lost. How old are you?"

"Fifteen."

"I just turned fourteen and you can do what I do."

"F-f-fourteen?" Mr. Martin asked in a surprised voice. "I thought you were sixteen or something."

"No."

"Holy cow," said Mr. Johnston, Sr.

"You afraid?" Jody the Boy one year older asked.

"Sort of." Truly, I felt afraid because I was cold and

shivering. But I also knew how to build a fire and I had enough food for three days. "I'm scared only because I know Mom is gonna be mad at me."

"Don't worry about that, k-k-kid," said Mr. Martin. "You saved us."

"Do you have children?' I asked him.

"F-f-four girls. Two sets of tw-tw-twins. Geenie and Judie are two. Lany and Lucy are four."

I could see that in my mind. He was a big man, like a bear. He stuttered and I felt that he was kind. I bet his girls had ringlets, big smiles and hung on him like a jungle gym.

"But how do you know where you're going?" Jody my Senior persisted.

"Map and compass."

"I don't know how to do that."

"It's easy. Get a book and learn. A compass costs less than five bucks."

"So, your mom taught you all this." He was quiet a few seconds. "My mom just stays at home and cleans house."

"Now Jody," his dad said. No wonder he said he'd talk to his son about women's roles after they got home.

"I bet she does a lot more than that," I said.

A few seconds of silence. Men tend to underestimate the amount of work housewives do. I cringed at the thought of what Mrs. Wabash had to put up with. Were there other Wabashes at home she was forced to deal with?

"Jody, I listen, pay attention and have spent my life outdoors. Mom wanted to be a lifeguard in high school so she took CPR and advanced first aid, both of which she renewed every year. Since she couldn't decide what to study in college, she didn't go for a semester and got her Emergency Medical Technician certificate. You can take classes at the Red Cross for almost nothing."

"I g-g-gotta go again," said Mr. Martin. He stood to go back to the woods.

"I do to," I said. "I'll get some more wood while I'm out." After climbing from the hole I waited for Mr. Martin to emerge from the dark forest then I intercepted him as he limped towards the hole.

"Mr. Martin," I said in a low voice.

"Yeah?"

"We have a problem."

"No k-k-kidding."

"I mean, Mr. Wabash. Has he had heart problems before?"

"What d-d-do you mean 'before'?"

"Looks like he's on the way to a heart attack, or maybe a stroke. My mother's father had these symptoms prior to his heart attack. Tell me what you know."

Mr. Martin took in and let out a frustrating breath. "Okay. It's like this. He's my brother in l-l-law. He's a smoker and a dr-dr-drinker and he never exercises. The only f-f-fruits and vegetables he eats are k-k-ketchup and carrot cake."

"Hmmm."

"Last year he had a mild str-str-stroke. He lost use of his r-r-right arm for a few days and then he recovered. He promised to st-st-start going to the gym and never did."

"Looks like his cough and tiredness may be the start of something."

"You think?"

"Yes."

"What sh-sh-should we do?"

"Don't say anything about it. Try and check on him during the night. How's your knee?" I asked.

"Sore."

"This is hard trip."

"I d-d-didn't know it would be."

So now we had several problems: a knee, an ankle, a lip and a potential heart attack or stroke. "If the snow's not too deep tomorrow then I'll go for help." I turned back to camp before he could object.

After we zipped our jackets, adjusted the hats onto our heads yet again and covered ourselves with garbage bags and tarps, I thought about Mom and where she might be this night. Was she crying with worry? Was she mad? Had she called to tell Dad I was missing?

Before I fell asleep to the sounds of the cold wind blowing through the tall pine tree tops, I said my nightly prayer. And as usual, I asked for help.

Chapter 11: Mr. Wabash

I sat through the night, awake for the most part. I was cold and worried. I had to take care of four people who had no idea what to do in their situation. And I was the fifth person, a young girl who wasn't sure if I was doing the right things. But I also had to consider that if I hadn't found these men, they probably would not have lived through the night.

Mom was right, as usual. Not all hunters are ignorant, but a lot of them are. Just yesterday morning before we left for the airport Pete kept asking Mom questions about the lost people.

"So who's lost?" Pete asked even though he heard what Sheriff Murray said. Nevertheless, he wanted to hear it again from Mom.

Mom sighed. "Well, Petie. Lost hunters."

"They're a pain."

"Yes sweetie. They can be a real pain if they're inexperienced. Some men often tend to be aggressive and concerned about their manhood, meaning they don't want to become humiliated over an unmanly situation. Such as finding themselves lost in the woods."

"Sort of like Dad," Pete said matter-of-factly.

"Why do you say that?" Mom asked.

"Because he's a man. Dad won't ask for directions if we're driving and he's not sure how to get to where he's going."

She chuckled. "A lot like Daddy, yes. Lost men in the woods behave the same way. They wander around until they end up where they want to be, then they don't tell anyone they were lost. Or they stay lost and die. At least if they die they don't have to feel humiliated."

"Women get upset when they're lost, too, you know," Pete argued. My baby brother has already figured out Mom's gender stereotypes.

"True. But at least they sit still as long as they don't have a man with them."

Mom likes to complain about lost hunters. "A lot of them act like they're great outdoorsmen," she's told me several times. "Some really are, but others know nothing about using a map and compass. They don't bring enough clothes, food and water. And, many of them don't tell anyone where they're going."

"They should," I'd agree.

Then she'd go on some more: "If you fall and break a leg or something, if no one knows where you are, then what? If you don't take a cell phone or walkie talkie, then how can you tell people about your position? Even if you have a cell phone, but if you have no idea how to read a map then how will rescuers know where to look if you can't tell them?"

"You can't," I'd answer.

She'd ignore me. "And, that's when your survival skills are supposed to help you out of the jam. But what if you have no survival skills?"

"You're in trouble," I'd say.

Mom is always determined to find the people she's looking for. Once she finds them, she's happy and satisfied. But I also know she tends to lecture them about safety. In some ways I felt sorry for the hunters because she gets madder about them than any other type of lost person. After Mom got through with them, they'd probably never go hunting again out of fear of having her come after them.

With that idea, I decided to move the tarp. But even before I even tried to peel the heavy blue tarp off of us, I knew that the ground was covered with snow. And a lot of it. I peeked out during the night to see heavy white flakes blowing sideways. The ground was covered with white and by the look of the snow on the tree branches, after mid-night at least four more inches had fallen.

Now the snow felt heavy. I was snug and warm where I lay on my side. Once I got up and moving all that would change. But it's not like I could get up and go into our nice warm den at home and turn on the t.v. There would be no hot chocolate or tea and no one would be around to pop me popcorn.

Then I thought about Mr. Wabash. I closed my eyes, said a quick prayer for the best, then opened them and focused on where he sat. He was still covered by the tarp, although his head with the stocking cap and the end of the orange bag was exposed.

"You awake?" Jody Sr. asked me. I thought not for the last time why anyone would name their kid their name. I recall that Dad made a comment once about how the boxer and grill guy, George Foreman, named all his kids George.

"Yep," I answered.

"I g-g-gotta go to the bathroom," said Mr. Martin.

"When you get up try not to spill snow down your coat or get it in your boots. It's heavy."

"Very heavy," agreed the Jr. Jody. "I kept looking out last night and it's about a foot deep."

"Well, it's almost two feet now." I said, "And it may be deeper in other places."

What I really meant was, it will be deeper. Not only that, it will be hard to walk through and the chances are great that someone will misstep and fall in a hole or will trip over something we can't see. After all, we were not on an established road. In fact, I didn't know the location of the established road. It was around here someplace, but where?

"Mr. Wabash?" I asked tentatively.

"He's okay, I th-th-think," Mr. Martin said quietly.

"I heard that," Mr. Wabash answered. He sounded sick and that dreaded chill went up my neck and into my temple. This meant my intuition warned me that our situation could go from bad to worse. I also knew a headache was on its merry way into my frontal lobe.

"How do you f-f-feel?" Mr. Martin asked him.

"Hungry. Cold. I gotta pee. I can't move my right arm."

"What?" I asked loudly. Sometimes I hate it when my intuition's right.

"It's numb. Dead. Can't feel it."

I noticed that he slurred his words. He sounded like my mouth feels after a trip to the dentist to get a deep cavity filled.

"Mr. Wabash," I said gently. "Can you take a deep breath?"

He inhaled, but coughed. "Hurts my ribs," he said.

"Can you move your legs?"

"Yeah." Jody Jr. moved the tarp away while his dad stood and tossed the accumulated snow out and over the edge of the hole. I watched as Mr. Wabash bent his knees. Mr. Martin unzipped the bag to reveal Mr. Wabash's legs.

"Oh, man." He grabbed his hurt ankle with his good hand. "My foot's dead too. But I can move my leg."

The left side of Mr. Wabash's face looked slack. A line of saliva stretched from the corner of his mouth to his chest. I ignored that for a moment.

As I moved the tarp I gave Mr. Martin a sideways glance. He nodded then took the tarp covered in snow and threw it out of the pit like Mr. Johnston did.

"Let me see your foot." What I saw shocked and scared me. The skin around the top edge of his boot had swollen up like warm yeasty bread. "The circulation's been cut off. Mr. Johnston, help me here."

Mr. Wabash tried to speak and instead managed a thick, wet cough.

We carefully pried the boot from Mr. Wabash's bloated foot. He moaned and cried out as the shoe came off. My wrap job had kept the foot stable, but the laces had cut off most of the circulation and his toes looked white. I pinched his cold, big toe and it barely changed color.

"Give me a knife," I ordered to the group.

"Why?" Mr. Wabash cried. "What are you gonna do?"

"I need to get this wrap off so your blood can flow to your toes."

"You said the tape would keep it stable." He coughed again.

"Yes I did. But you weren't supposed to lace up your boot real tight on top of the tape."

"I thought that it would be better in my boot. Last night I put it on."

I didn't reply. "We're gonna stay out here 'til we die," he slurred. Maybe now you see why I got tired of listening to him.

"I never thought the trip would end up like this," Mr. Johnston said, a bit of water pooling in his eyes. Dark circles had formed under his eyes and he looked tried and frail. His lips were chapped and he needed some heavy moisturizer on his red, dry cheeks.

"L-l-listen, if you guys get out of here, t-t-tell my wife and k-k-kids I love them," said Mr. Martin. His big ol' moustache had frost on it.

"It's okay, son," I heard Big Jody say to worried Little Jody. "We'll get out of this all right. She knows what she's doing."

That made me feel somewhat better, but at the moment Mr. Wabash was in a world of trouble.

"My head hurts, dad," the Jody Jr. said.

"There's Motrin my fanny pack," I said. "Break one in half and take it. While I'm doing this, you others get that fire going."

This day started clear, crispy and white. Even though the clouds were gone and the sun slowly rose through the trees to make the day warmer, we still had serious worries ahead. Trudging through snow can be tiring and dangerous. I knew that we didn't have to go anywhere, that sitting still would be the best. I knew where we were in relation to the base camp, but it was miles across tough terrain.

"Wait. Who's got gaiters?" I asked them as I held Mr. Wabash's cold, injured foot in my warmer hands.

"What are gaiters?" Mr. Wabash asked as quietly as a mouse.

"Gaiters are leg wraps that you can zip but usually tie on over your shoes up to your knees so that snow can't work its way into your footwear. Mom and I wear mini gaiters over our running shoes when it snows in Oklahoma. Snow's not so deep there so mini gaiters only come up a bit past our ankles." I didn't need to wonder if he had a pair.

"I got a pair," said Mr. Martin.

"That all? No one else?" I sniffed and wiped my nose with my hand. "Well, I got one pair. I also have a pair of Gore Tex foot covers."

They all looked at me. I pulled the wadded Gore Tex socks from my pack and tossed them to Small Jody. "They're like socks but are waterproof. Jody Jr., you wear those. Your boots may get wet but these will keep your feet dry. Take off your socks. Put these waterproof ones on so they'll be underneath them."

"Hey, thanks."

"Thanks Tuli," said his dad.

I may only be fourteen, but it was obvious to me that Jimmy's dad was feeling unhappy at this moment. I mean, parents are supposed to protect their kids, not get them into situations like this. He looked ashamed of himself.

"How's the lip?"

"Hurts."

"Get a snow ball and hold it on there for a minute. You got lip balm?"

"Yeah, I got a tube here." He patted his coat breast pocket.

"Keep putting that on all day. This cold weather will dry you out fast and your cut will be painful if it splits any more."

"I'll do it," he promised.

"Mr. Johnston, can you get that fire going?" I asked.

The three males started to scramble out from their hole. "Wait!" I yelled. "We need to make just one entrance. Otherwise you'll pull all the snow into the pit and it'll make mud. Come over here and let's push the snow away so we have a path."

I set Mr. Wabash's foot down and wrapped it in his sweatshirt.

We worked hard to get the snow moved aside. After fifteen minutes I felt sweaty. "Everyone stop," I said. "Are you sweating?"

The group nodded. "Take off a layer. Or else as soon as we stop we'll get chilled."

"Yeah, okay," agreed Mr. Martin.

"You have a wrap for that knee?" I asked.

"An ace bandage."

"When you get home, ask about a brace for when you do this kind of activity."

"I d-d-don't plan on doing this again."

"Oh, don't think like that," I said. "If you have your gear together it could be fun."

No one had a comment for that. Considering our situation, my fun comment did sound pretty lame.

They climbed out of the hole and found that the snow rose to their knees. Or should I say they sank up to their knees? Anyway, deep snow is not a good thing.

I turned back to Mr. Wabash's foot. I cut off the wrap and lay his foot in my lap. It didn't look pretty. I doubt that it looked pretty even when uninjured. Anyway, it had tried to swell even more during the night and his skin was deeply creased from the tape that kept the swelling in check. Worse, the foot was pale. I ran my fingernails across the sole.

"Feel that?"

"No."

I scratched the top of his foot in the same way. "What about now?"

"No."

Then I pinched his heel and moved his foot at the ankle. He jumped. "Yes! Stop! I felt that. It hurts."

"Good." I put on his sock and then wrestled on the boot. I set his foot down and draped his Hanes sweatshirt over it. "Don't move," I ordered.

I put on my gaiters then climbed from the hole to join the others around the fire pit. They hadn't done much except to make a trail. I untied the branches that we had draped over the pit and they watched me shake snow off the rope. Then I looped the rope up in a wrapped-and-reef knotted coil.

I knew the men focused on me. I didn't look up when I told them, "This way the rope won't get tangled in my pack. This is a good way to coil up extension cords." I tossed it into the hole where I'd pack it later.

"Listen," I said quietly to get their attention. "Mr. Wabash had a stroke. He can't be moved so y'all will need stay here and keep this fire going. Start another one in the hole. I'll leave as much equipment and food as I can for you."

"You're n-n-not going out there b-b-by yourself," Mr. Martin said in the same tone of voice my dad uses.

"No ma'am, you certainly are not," agreed Mr. Johnston.

I didn't want to go out by myself in snow. That was for certain. But I also knew I had to find help. So I said, "Look, there's no trail and there's no way they're going to find us. These trees are so thick they can't see our smoke. And it's so windy a helicopter could get in trouble if it tries to fly over. I know where we are and I know where to go."

"You want m-m-me to go with you?" Mr. Martin asked.

"No." I may have said that too quickly. "I mean, normally I'd like the company, but the snow would tear up your knee. You need to stay here and help keep Mr. Wabash warm. If he has another stroke he may die. He may have a heart attack. His foot looks bad and it feels cold."

"Then let's all go," Mr. Johnston said. "We'll make a litter and drag him."

"No," I said.

"Why not?"

"He's too heavy. Look, when searchers evacuate an injured person it takes six men, three on each side to carry that person out on a litter. And, the carriers are supposed to switch sides every few minutes because it's harder than you think to carry a person with one hand. There're only two adults and two kids here to help."

"But we'll drag him, not carry him," Mr. Johnston argued.

"Yeah, I know. But it's too far. I know where the operations site is. About two or three miles from here. If the ground was clear, then it would be easy to walk it. But there's almost two feet of snow on the ground. We'd be exhausted pulling him in after twenty feet because we have to break a trail. Plus, we have our packs to carry."

"Maybe s-s-she's right," said Mr. Martin. "We won't have the energy t-t-to dig in if we need to."

Mr. Johnston nodded his head towards me. "Yeah, but neither will she after a day of hiking."

"Don't worry about me. I got all the right gear and I can handle things if it's just me. If I think I'm getting lost then I'll stay put. But I know where we are."

Now, I sure sound confident, right? Actually, I was scared and knew that I could be in a huge crisis if I hurt myself. On the other hand, Mr. Wabash was fading and could die if he didn't get attention in a hurry.

"Man, it's bright out here," said Little Jody. He heard our conversation and it frightened him. So he focused on something else.

"Sure is," I agreed. "You got sunglasses?"

"I don't, but my dad does."

"We need to put them on. You have a face mask, Jody?"

"A black one. Why?"

"If the sky's clear today, then the sun will reflect off the snow right into your eyes. If you don't block it somehow, you may get snow blindness. That mask will help because it'll keep the light from bouncing off your cheeks."

"My cheeks?"

"Well, that and the skin under your eyes. Why do you think football players put black stuff under their eyes?"

"Oh. I never thought about that."

"You think they all had black eyes?"

Mr. Martin laughed at that.

"Okay. Let's get a move on that fire. We need to clear all the snow out and as much from around the edge of the pit as we can. The heat will melt the snow and you'll end up with a mush pit."

The truth is, I had precious little experience in cold weather. I was actually making this up as I went along.

Mr. Wabash sat in the sleeping hole while the rest of us worked hard to move the snow away from the pit. We alternated using our hands, the two camping cups and the small cooking pot as scoops. After half an hour we cleared away enough snow to safely start the fire.

"We can drink melted snow. We have to make sure it's boiled first. No telling what pollution it fell through before it landed here. I have tea bags for flavor."

"You need to t-t-take the p-p-pot with you, Tuli," Mr. Martin said. "You have to stay warm, t-t-too."

"No, you keep it. I got my heavy cup that I can heat. Look, I can move pretty fast and should get some help in a few hours." I think. Well, at least that's what I told him. I figured I'd go pretty darn slow.

We made breakfast of hot tea, granola bars, beef jerky and a few dried apricots. I took part of the cheese hunk, the half-pound of smoked salmon and a can of Beenie Weenies. I left them the dried milk, macaroni, spaghetti sauce and the cans of corn. I tossed in my baggies of spices and a few packs of Motrin.

I filled my two bottles with hot tea and put one inside my jacket to keep me warm, and the other I wore in my fanny pack underneath my jacket in hopes that would stay warm as well. I filled Mr. Martin's Pepsi bottle and put that in a breast pocket. All in all, I had enough food for two lean days.

"Stay in the hole as much as you can," I told them. "Keep warm. Especially keep Mr. Wabash warm. That wood won't last long so someone has to go find more. Put it in the pit standing up length-ways. You know, vertical, so the heat from the fire can dry it out. Make a big pile so you can keep the wood drying on an assembly line."

I hefted my big pack and fastened it around my waist. The bulk of my fanny pack rested against my abdomen and snapped behind my back.

"You g-g-gonna be okay?" Mr. Martin asked in a low voice. I knew he was truly worried, but he also was smart enough to know I had to leave and find help.

"Yes. I'll be fine."

My hands were shaking and I thought I'd be sick. I was scared and sure I'd never see my family again. The landscape was white and everything looked the same. And it was very, very quiet. Could I make it? I had no intuition about this at all.

"Have Jody Jr. sit close to Mr. Wabash all day and night," I said. "Keep both of them covered and their hats on. Keep drinking warm water. Help Mr. Wabash keep his foot warm by putting it on one of your stomachs."

"Huh?" That was a question from Jody Sr.

"That's the warmest place for his foot. If it warms up too fast by a fire it'll hurt him worse than spraining it again. Don't bother retaping his ankle. He shouldn't put any weight on it anyway. Put it back in the boot and wrap his sweatshirts around it."

Mr. Martin gave me a hug. Then the Jodys hugged me. Mr. Wabash held out his good hand. I took it and felt tears in my eyes.

"Thanks kid," he said.

"No problem. I'll be back." Then to the others: "Do not follow me." I said loudly. "You'll only get lost. Promise."

"Promise," Mr. Martin repeated.

"It won't be long. Trackers are already looking for you. You don't have to go anywhere."

"We understand."

I sure hoped they did. If anyone one of them felt heroic and came after me, this entire fiasco would take on new meaning.

"You'll do great," said Jody Jr. He gave me another thumb's up, just like my brother does.

When I smiled I felt my lip crack. Darn. Where did I put that lip balm?

As long as I had water and my gear, I'd stay warm. At least that's what I kept telling myself as I headed north into the woods of the snowy North Rim.

Chapter 12: On My Own

"A little farther. A little more." I encouraged myself as I pushed through the powder.

My body needed a rest after three hours of tough trudging and carrying the heavy pack. I'd marched through the thick snow slowly and deliberately to save my energy, stopping to catch my breath every ten minutes. My leg hurt, my muscles burned and the silence pounded in my ears. Actually, I think it was my heartbeat, but the silence was so complete that I started wondering if this was what silence sounded like.

I found the hill where I'd seen Jody Jr's. blood and it looked like the snow hadn't stopped the deer from locating their game trail. Their distinct tracks wound through the trees and I wondered if they were tired from breaking trail.

The snow shined like tiny jewels. The millions of ice crystals sparkled a variety of colors and if I stared at the sea of bright white without my sunglasses I'd quickly go blind and get the biggest headache of my life.

I kicked away snow around some fallen trees and cleared away a spot to sit. I poured the crumbled granola bar into my mouth and swallowed some tea. I shouldn't drink tea because it draws moisture from your tissues and can make you even thirstier. But at least the tea tasted better than plain old warm water.

Who drinks warm water, anyway? Oh, never mind. My grandpa did in the mornings to make him go potty.

By this time I felt tired and wanted to lay still wrapped in warm blankets drinking hot chocolate with marshmallows, but from watching my mom over the years I knew I had to stay alert and ready to work. Fatigue and stress are realities of search and rescue. And so is fighting the stress that goes along with trying to find lost, possibly injured adults and children. Mom is good at what she does because she's able to concentrate and work even if she's hungry, sore and tired.

"Mommy, don't you get lost now," I had said to my Mom yesterday morning in the kitchen. I giggled as I said it. Mom never gets lost and at the time I thought it was a funny thing to say. "I don't want to have to come find you." I had been excited to go and felt silly.

"I doubt you'll have to do that, honey," she said.

Even if she did somehow lose her way, Mom would stop and stay where she was. Then she would use all the gear in her well-stocked pack to keep warm. She'd eat chocolate bars and dried fruit. She would read the paperback she always carries in the outer pocket of her pack until rescuers arrived.

"And what are the rules if you get lost?" She asked me and Pete that a hundred times so we'd always remember what to do in the unlikely event we found ourselves separated from her or a group in the woods.

"Stay put," I said.

"But before that," Pete said, "You should have told people where you were going. And you have to be prepared for bad weather."

"Right," Mom agreed.

"I'll never get lost," Pete announced.

"I certainly hope not, son," Mom said.

I wished I had the dogs with me. I'd never had the chance to do a real search with them, although I'd trained with them a lot. "This search would have gone a whole lot smoother if the dogs hadn't stepped in barbed wire," I said to the white landscape.

John would have worked the best for me. She's interesting in that she'll mind me and will always follow the tracking patterns that she learned during several thousands of hours of training. But she has her own mind and her little doggy brain often comes up with new ideas. Although she doesn't act on all her thoughts, she alerts me and Mom to them.

Like two years ago when Mom, John and Happy were sent to find a three-year-old boy who wandered off from his parent's camp at Possum Kingdom Lake west of Fort Worth.

"I followed the kid's obvious Teva sandal tracks for two miles," Mom told us with her mouth full of spinach salad later that evening. "We were close to the shore and the water from the lake made the ground mushy and filled in the tracks and I couldn't see them anymore. I felt certain that kid wandered down hill into some trees. Happy acted like she had no idea where he went, but John stopped and looked the other direction, up the hill."

Pete smacked his lips as he ate a ripe peach. "John always knows," Pete said.

"Sure enough," Mom agreed. "The wind blew away from us and a light rain started. That made it difficult for both dogs to scent. John looked back at me, then up the hill. She sat and waited for me to make a decision."

"And so what did you do, Mommy?" asked Pete. He loves Mom's stories.

"Well,' I said, 'I don't think he went up there, John. A kid couldn't climb through that.' But John just looked up the hill again then back at me.

"So I said, 'shoot. Okay, John. Go.' You know how she is," Mom laughed. "John made her way through the rocks and brambles, which is not surprising. She acts like obstacles are character-developing challenges. I held my arms across my face to keep from getting cut."

Now, Happy is pretty sure footed, but she doesn't like challenges very much so I wasn't surprised to hear that she hung back. During obstacle training, John runs right across ladders and drainage pipes while Happy acts like she's stepping on hot coals.

Mom continued. "John couldn't smell very well with the wind and rain. Man, that dog was determined to go over the rocks so I humored her. We finally got away from the brambles and found that lost kid sitting on a rock, a smile on his face. He was holding a two-foot water snake that curled around his arm. When we got back to camp, the little boy's mother cried and hugged her cold, wet kid then she thanked me. Then his dad spanked him."

Mom speared some of her steamed asparagus and nibbled the end of it. Pete did the same. "Human nature amazes me," Mom said. "What a jerk."

I don't think that all people are jerks, but as I grow older and encounter more people—and some of those folks I've met under stressful circumstances--I realize more and more that human nature really is amazing.

A raven caw-cawed at me from a high branch. I clucked at him, or maybe it was a her, then asked how she was doing. "*Halito, Fala chito. Chim achukma?*- Hello Raven. How are you?"

"Caw. Caw," she replied.

"*Sa hohchifo ut Tuli.*- My name is Tuli."

"Caw. Caw."

"*Llappa hikia ka hopakil?*- Is it far from here?"

"Caw. Caw."

"*Sa pisachi.*- Show me."

Raven took off from her branch and flew to another one, in a slightly different direction from where I was heading. I thought I was going north. Maybe not. Clouds gathered to blot out the sun. *Fala chito* flew from branch to branch, looking back at me at each pause.

Some birds, like ravens, crows and owls, are considered to be bad luck by some Indians. I, on the other hand, prefer to judge each animal on an individual basis. I decided to trust this one.

Ravens tend to travel in very small groups or alone. Maybe she decided that I'd be her partner for a few days.

I felt winded and sweaty, not a good thing to feel in cold weather. I only had one other shirt to wear under my heavy sweater and I couldn't afford to become chilled. Raven looked down at me from her perch. My wind-burned lips ached.

"*Sa itukshila.*" Actually, I felt very thirsty.

I stopped to take a swig of water only to realize I had just one swallow left in that bottle.

Despite the tall trees that blocked a good portion of the sky from view I could tell that sun set grew close. I estimated it to be around five o'clock. I had probably come about half-way to Operations camp. How could it have taken me so long to get to this point? I turned around and looked at the crooked trail I made behind me. It meandered side to side. If I had indeed wandered like this all day, no wonder it took me so long to travel just a few miles. In Oklahoma I could have run that distance in less than thirty minutes.

To make matters more interesting, dark clouds began to gather and it smelled like snow again. I mean, snow was all over the ground, but I could smell more on the wind. This meant that I'd have to deal with yet another night under my tarp being covered with snow.

I broke off two good-sized branches from a dead Ponderosa and hit them against the tree trunk a few times to lose the snow. I carried the dry wood over my shoulder with the intention of using it to start my fire.

When I stopped for the night I felt tired, hungry and dizzy. If I waited any longer I'd be too tired to dig a shelter and make a fire. After trudging through the deep snow for hours, I wondered if my body had enough energy to dig through it.

I found a spot on the ground under thick branches where the snow wasn't as deep. I took off my pack then used my foot to push snow back. Have you ever pushed snow around with your foot? It's hard work. I used my cup and scooped out more snow until metal hit dirt. I worked hard until I had created a space about three by four feet.

Plenty of downed, dead wood lay under the snow. I pulled out some pieces and lay them in a pile after brushing away the deep snow. I rummaged around for more until I found enough for a small fire that could burn for maybe an hour. That wasn't enough, so I didn't stop to rest until I'd gathered another two hours' worth.

I broke up the wood I'd been carrying into smaller pieces for kindling. With help from my trusty BIC lighter my fire sputtered to life. I boiled snow in my little cup. I chowed down on half the salmon and one can of corn. Talk about hungry! I could have eaten ten times more. There was only a small amount of food left, so as the snow started to fall I settled for warm water and a good tooth flossing.

There's no television in the woods and many people think they'll become bored on a camping trip. But really, there are all kinds of things to occupy yourself with. Bird and animal watching, photography, and reading in a hammock strung between two trees. Finding wood and digging a latrine help to make a person comfy. Of course, if you're stuck in the woods trying to survive, the activity really never ends except when you finally sleep.

But sleeping doesn't come easy when you're overtired and nervous about what might happen next. I'd made my fire, ate my meager dinner, drank three cups of warm water and wondered what Pete was doing. Probably eating pizza while watching "Sponge Bob" and reading *Harry Potter* all at the same time.

Then I suddenly remembered that tonight was my date with Shawn. Did he ask someone else? I figured that my leaving town in combination with ruining the *kapucha* game last spring would make him forget me pretty quick. I felt sad, but also realized that I was getting used to feeling down.

I still felt thirsty and that worried me. I shivered even though the fire burned only six inches from my legs. I found another wool cap in my pack and put that on over my navy blue one. Heat escapes through your head, so hopefully mine would stay warm with two layers.

My knee hurt and I knew that tomorrow my entire leg would ache. I took out my last pack of Motrin and swallowed both of them. I hoped I wouldn't get a stomach ache taking them with out also having a belly full of food.

Now I was hungry again and coyotes howled. They sounded close. The tricksters were out and about as usual, but I wasn't worried about them. Unless they're starving or diseased they would leave me alone. Just to make certain though, I put my food in a garbage bag and tied one end of my rope around it. I selected a tree thirty feet from where I'd sleep, then threw the bag over a twenty-foot high branch and tied the other end of the rope to a lower branch. They'd be attracted to the salmon package and hopefully, would stay away from me.

I stared into the fire, wishing I had marshmallows, graham crackers and a Hershey bar. With that thought, I fell asleep.

"Caw Caw."

I woke to the sound of *Fala chito* calling. She perched directly above me on a low branch. Although my fire had long since gone out in the night, I felt surprisingly warm wrapped inside my clothes and tarp.

The morning was once again bright and cold. Three more inches of snow had dropped over night and I noticed that my trail from the day before had been covered. If Mom had crossed my path, she wouldn't know it now.

I took my bottle from where I stashed it next to my warm chest under my long underwear, sweater, vest and jacket. On any other day, warm melted snow water would taste pretty terrible, but this morning it woke me up and got my blood moving.

Raven received a bite of smoked salmon and a few kernels of corn from my light breakfast. Then she flew to a branch twenty feet away and waited for me. "Caw Caw."

I stood and felt stiff. My knee didn't hurt but my thigh sure did. I walked the only way I could through the deep snow: slowly.

As I looked around, I noticed coyote tracks all around my camp. One came close enough to smell my head. Luck was on my side, though. True to their reputation as skittish scavengers, I was left alone. But I did feel a pang of fear. A pack of wild animals lurking close by is not a pretty thought for a lone child out in the wilderness. Of course, coyotes travel alone or with just a few others, but still, I felt concern that they were here.

As far as I could see were trees and snow. The sun shone through the trees in the east, which meant I needed to go a bit more to the right to make sure I got close to the junction of 447 and 252.

"Caw Caw," *Fala chito* yelled.

"Now what?" I trudged forward for another hour and half-a-mile. My legs felt like lead blocks and my head throbbed. I thought of Mr. Wabash and kept going for another twenty minutes.

Fala chito cawed again and I stopped. Right in front of me was a bright pink string stretched across the trail. At seven foot intervals along the string were small pieces of paper, folded over and stapled onto the line. Each yellow paper had an arrow drawn on it.

"Mom." I said out loud. This is a strategy she told me about only last month. In stringing a line across a likely path the lost person might take, that person can follow the strings and arrows to the trail.

Since the arrows pointed the way I was headed, I knew that Mom had enough confidence in me to find the string. That is, I was close to the trail because of my own brain power. Or to be pessimistic, she thought I might stumble onto it by accident. I hoped it was the first.

The string went a long way, about a quarter of a mile. The yellow sticky intervals grew farther apart. Mom must have been in short supply. Finally, the string stopped at a large Ponderosa that stood next to a trail packed down by numerous feet and snowmobile runners. Raven took in the scene from her perch high above me.

I caught the faint odor of food cooking. Almost there, I kept telling myself.

On I went, seemingly endlessly. By my watch it was only another thirty minutes, but it felt like hours. Finally, there I stood panting like a race horse, at the edge of Operations camp and no one saw me. The Operations table was about thirty feet away, with people crowding around the table, looking at the map. More emergency vehicles with uniformed personnel had arrived before the snow had fallen. I could tell because snow covered their bumpers.

I recognized one of the trucks that belonged to one of the hunters whose camp I had found. I was probably right. They got my note and left camp to tell someone.

Mom stood at the table, arguing with someone. No doubt about which way to go and where to look. She had just come back from an ATV run by the looks of her wind-blown hair. I looked to the large cook fire area where a dozen people stood around eating off of paper plates.

A tall man and young boy stood with their hands in the pockets of their down vests. Dad and Pete. What were they doing here?

I walked closer until I caught the attention of a man dressed in a hot shot uniform drinking from a white cup. His eyes grew large then he nudged the woman next to him with his elbow. By then, half the people around the table turned to see what the deal was.

I trudged closer. "Hi Mom," I said after I reached the table. I felt like a marathoner crossing the finish line 10 hours after the winner had already gone home. My throat felt sore and scratchy and my lips were dried and cracked.

Mom usually keeps herself under careful control, but when she saw me she almost knocked down the table to get to me.

"*Sioshitek!*-My daughter. Baby, baby," she cried as she hugged me the best she could, considering I had on my big pack and fanny pack. "Oh, honey, where were you? I thought I lost you." She cried openly and I thought I heard a few sniffs from the table.

She helped me unbuckle and drop my packs then she held my face in her hands. "Are you okay?" Are you hurt? Frostbite?" She grabbed my gloved hands and tore off my gloves to see if my fingers were pink or white.

Dad, Pete, Rowdy and Mickey sprinted over to me through the snow. Rowdy hugged me hard.

"You look healthy, kid," Rowdy said.

"I'm okay." I coughed. My throat was dry. "I found the hunters."

"Tuli," yelped Pete. He hit me in the arm. "I knew you'd show up." Actually, my brother didn't look like he was worried. Now Dad, on the other hand . . .

My father picked me up and held me in the air. My ribs hurt where his hands dug into my sides. "Honey, honey," Dad kept saying. His hair was uncombed and stuck up and out on the sides, much like Pete's does. Tears ran down his cheeks.

"Geez, Dad," said Pete. "Put her down." He turned to me and put his hands on his hips. "So you found 'em? Where are they?"

"What?" Mickey said as he pushed his way to me.

"I found them." My words felt heavy and slow. "I'll show you on the map. Mr. Wabash had a stroke," I said quietly so the others couldn't hear. "He turned his ankle really bad and that's why I left by myself. Mom, he may not make it."

"Show us," Mickey said. "Then we'll have a doctor look at you."

I showed the people around the table where I left the lost hunters. Then Mickey got on the radio to alert the riders who were already in the field, then he, Rowdy and a dozen other snow mobilers took off like a hoard of Chevy engines at the Indy 500.

"Baby, my baby," Mom continued to cry. She led me to a large trailer equipped with a wonderful heater and hot water for a shower. Half a dozen other people, four men and two women crowded in with us. Two were firemen but the other folks wore uniforms I didn't recognize.

"What happened?" Dad asked when we got settled in the warm trailer. I smiled at his messed up hair.

Another guy came in with a tray of hot food. Fried chicken, mashed potatoes and corn on the cob are my favorites, but Mom rarely allows me and Pete to eat grease or butter.

"Eat," Mom ordered.

"Okay. Looks good."

"Can I have some?" Pete asked. Dad handed him a bag of bagels from a box of supplies that sat on the floor.

"Where did you go after it rained?" Mom tightly held my right hand and I found it hard to eat with my left.

"It rained so hard I couldn't see anything in front of me. So I dug in and stayed put." I took a huge bite of potato with yummy gravy. I craved spice and so I dumped more salt and pepper onto the brown sauce. After long hikes and especially after I've sweated a lot, I also want white onions. "Any onions?"

Pete looked in the bread box and pulled out a purple one. Dad took it and my knife and started cutting it.

Everyone in the trailer watched me. "I found the men's tracks the next morning and I followed. "What did you do?" I asked Mom. Dad handed me a slice of onion and I put the entire thing in my mouth.

"I tried to find your tracks and I did pretty well until it got dark. I dug in like you did that night and came back around midnight. It was the hardest thing I ever did, leaving you out there."

"But Mom," I responded with a louder voice. "You know I had a full pack and could deal with a little storm."

She just stared at me a few seconds. "But it was pouring and cold. And you're my daughter."

The others nodded. "I'd be a raving maniac if my daughter was out there alone," said one of the firemen.

"How are the dogs?"

"Fine," Mom answered. "There're at a vet in Page."

"Yup," the man standing behind repeated, "if it were my kid, I'd be looney tunes about now.

"Ha ha!" blurted Pete. "Looney Tunes!"

"Son," Dad said. "Quiet."

Mom ignored him. "I went out the next day until the ATV almost was out of gas. I had to come back to fill up. Then I went back. I stayed out that night as the snow fell. The ATV had a harder time when the snow got deeper. Several other people got stuck and had to hike back."

"Other people were looking for me?" I crammed a roll in my mouth.

Mom looked to the others and sighed. "Yes, honey. A lot. You left a note in a camp and the hunters came to Jacob Lake Inn to report it. At least I knew you were okay late yesterday morning."

"Are they okay?"

"One got frostbite on his toes and another fell off his ATV and broke his leg."

I chewed slowly. I felt sick. Man, what is it with ATV riders who keep falling off? They aren't that hard to ride. "Mom, they didn't need to come after me. I was okay. I am okay."

"Yeah, and you're fourteen," said a woman in what I thought might be a police uniform. How many people could fit into this trailer?

"I thought it would be a good idea to get Dad out here. So we called him. Lincoln made the arrangements."

"Yeah, and I got to come," Pete said as he chomped on his bagel. "I barfed in the plane."

"Yes, son," said Dad. "You certainly did."

Pete smiled big like he was proud of himself.

Another man dressed like a fireman brought me cup of hot chocolate. A Black woman came in the trailer behind him wearing heavy-duty winter clothes, a short hair-do and bright earrings. She put her hand on my shoulder.

"I'm Dr. Lacy Burnett," she said in gentle voice, like she was afraid she'd find something wrong with me. "Let's take a look at you."

Dr. Burnett did a quick appraisal and was satisfied that my feet and hands were not frostbitten. I told her what I ate and drank the past few days and the onlookers murmured their approval.

"Good thinking, kid," one old man said. "Not many adults could have handled being out there alone." How come everyone calls me 'kid?'

"Tuli, tell me more about the hunters." Mom asked.

I looked around me. "Their family here?"

"No, not yet," the old man said. "The wives are at the Jacob Lake Inn where it's warm. You can tell us."

So, I told them about finding the lost men and what we did to survive the cold, snowy night. I talked about Mr. Wabash and how he insisted on hiking out, despite his injury. They asked questions about what the men were wearing, what we ate and if they seemed capable of surviving the night.

"I don't know. Maybe," I answered. "I left as much food as I could spare and made sure they had fuel to keep a fire going. They're in a good sized hole in the ground and they know to keep the tarp over them. Little Jody has a badly split lip. Almost completely through the whole lip down to his chin. Mom, I kept telling him that you could sew him up."

Mom barely smiled at that. She squeezed my hand instead.

"You did fine, baby," Dad said as he reached over to take my hand. "You need to lay down. Try and sleep for a while and then you can take a shower."

"I'd do better with a shower first. Oh wait." I put some chicken, a bit of roll and a corn cob on a napkin. "I have to do something else first."

I stood and went to the door. "Mom, Dad, Pete. Come with me."

"What are you doing?" Pete asked.

"It's important." I went outside with my food. I went back to where I entered the camp.

"*Fala chito!*" I called.

"You found a raven." Mom didn't seem too surprised. "I saw one too."

"Hey wait for me!" Yelled my brother.

"Caw Caw." Raven called from the branches above us

"And there she is," Pete yelled again.

I set the food down and backed off a few feet. "*Yakoke-*Thanks."

Raven caw-cawed once before landing next to her lunch.

I don't usually like seeing adults upset, but this time I didn't mind watching Mom and Dad cry like babies.

Chapter 13: End of the Day

Only a few purple clouds floated across the emerald-green sky, but thunder boomed continually and bolts of red lightning hit the yellow ground, causing chunks of orange and pink clods of earth to be thrown a mile high into the air where they turned into balloons and drifted away. A flock of maroon ravens sat among the tree branches and fluffy blue leaves and caw-cawed with opera voices while a pack of rust-colored coyotes howled the Britney Spears' song, "Oops, I Did It Again," in the tall brush that burned with silver flames.

Then all was quiet. The thunder, ravens and coyotes became silent and their noise was replaced by the cheering of the search and rescue people who watched the Johnstons, Mr. Martin and Mr. Wabash play *kapucha* at the bottom of Meteor Crater, 30 miles east of Flagstaff. The lost hunters dressed in the same clothes worn by the elves in Lord of the Rings, while the spectators dressed like Johnny Depp in "Pirates of the Caribbean." Mr. Wabash ran along the rock-strewn crater floor easily as he caught the leather ball and scored one point after the other.

He waved and I waved back.

Then Mom walked up behind me in her calico dress and white apron, the traditional dress she wears during Choctaw celebrations. She wore no shoes, and a knife stuck up from the arch of her foot like Excalibur in the Stone.

"Mom," I said. "You were supposed to go to the doctor and get that knife out of your foot."

"Yeah, I know. But I'll need forty stitches and won't be able to run."

"That's for sure. Are you trying to teach me a lesson or something?"

She shrugged then said, "I know what its like to have to sit still, not being able to use an arm, a leg, or even my head. And I also know that the next time I slice a pie in my bare feet I should hold the knife tighter."

"I'll never get in shape," I mumbled.

"Time goes by quickly. In the meantime, use my bike."

I woke up with a start. I can't recall most dreams, but this dream had a lot of details and it made my head hurt. I rubbed my leg with both hands and took a few breaths. My hands went to my ear lobes and I was happy to find that both my spider earrings had made it with me through the difficult week. I looked at the clock and it said eleven o'clock.

My head felt groggy as I dragged myself into the kitchen.

"How'd you sleep, sweetie?" Dad asked me.

"Okay. My lips hurt." They felt hot and dry despite the Vaseline I coated them with before I went to bed. Happy and John lay on the floor with their front feet wrapped. Happy's long tail flipped back and forth while John's stubby tail moved in a circle.

I went to the dogs and sat on the floor with my hands on their heads. John whined.

"What about your leg?" Dad asked as he cooked scrambled eggs and vegetables.

"Aches. It's hard walking through snow."

"I bet it does," said Pete. "You should have had snowshoes."

I heard Mom crying last night before I fell asleep. The pressure she felt to find me was great and she no doubt felt the same emotional and physical pains I did from struggling through the deep snow.

"Did I hear the doorbell ring this morning or was I dreaming?"

"You weren't dreaming," Brother Pete said. He had spooned so much Malt-o-Meal into his mouth that his cheeks puffed out like a squirrel gathering nuts for the winter. "You got those flowers over there." He pointed to the den with his spoon. "Looks like Mom's garden."

From where I sat in the kitchen, the front room looked more like a flower shop. "Who sent those?"

"Well, let's see." Dad had the cards on the kitchen counter. His hair lay flat and he didn't have that scared look any more. "Those lilies are from Mickey. Actually, they're to you and Mom. The spring bouquet is from Jacob Lake Fire Department. And the daisies are from a Mrs. Wabash. Her card reads, 'Thank you for saving my baby.'"

"Her baby?" I laughed. "That kid's last name was Johnston."

"I don't think that's who she's referring to," Mom said.

"Mr. Wabash?"

"If the shoe fits," she answered.

"Tell her about the roses, Dad," said Pete.

Dad smiled and brought the roses in a green glass vase to the table. He handed me the small envelope attached to a stem. I opened it and read.

"Read it out loud,' Pete said. "Who's it from?" He smirked and I knew he already knew the answer to that.

I elbowed him in the side. "I think you know who it's from."

I took a breath and read aloud the messy handwriting: "To Tuli. You did a good job. Let's go to the game next week. Your friend, Shawn. And my parents."

Dad snickered. Mom gave him a sharp look. "That's nice, honey," she said.

"You and Mom got some more flowers from the tribe," Pete said. "And some guy called to get some information about what happened because he's gonna put it on the Choctaw web site."

"And this came, too." Dad handed me a big white envelope. I opened it to find a greeting card that said 'congratulations' on the cover. On the inside of the card were dozens of signatures. They were all from my *kapucha* team. I looked at the little notes each person wrote.

"I am so proud of you," Love Arnie.

"Way to go," Love Jen.

Then other notes, like "come home soon," you're my hero," and things like that.

"They did that after they found out you went on the search," Dad said. "Instead of going to school or to the game they went to Shawn's house to keep track of the search. His dad has that radio that can find stations in Russia. They got to hear the entire episode."

"You mean, my friends heard everything that was said at the Operation table?"

"Yes," Mom answered. "Even the conversations you had with those men who were hurt. And with me. Then they listened the entire time you were missing."

"The newspaper people were here, too," Pete said. He licked the bowl and reached for the oatmeal cookies. "Dad told them to go away."

"Newspaper?" I asked. This seemed like part of the weird dream I just had.

Dad poured himself more coffee and dumped in a few seconds worth of sugar. "They want an interview and I told them you were sleeping."

"Why do they want to talk to me? I mean, didn't Mom deal with them last night?"

Well, I thought she dealt with it. Coming home was a blur.

After I had returned to the Operations camp, I went through almost more activity than when I was breaking through the snow. The snowmobiles returned with Mr. Wabash, Mr. Martin and the

Johnstons. All four were weary and tired, but none were frostbitten. When I heard the snowmobiles come into camp I burst out the trailer door and ran to see what they brought back. I'd be lying if I said Mr. Wabash hadn't been on my mind.

As I predicted, Mr. Wabash's foot was still swollen. Luckily for him, his friends kept him warm and hydrated with warm water. Jody Jr's. lip looked bad. The split appeared crusty and oozy at the same time. Without medical intervention he might end up with a V-shaped bottom lip.

"Oh my," said Dr. Burnett. "That's gonna need some major help."

"I should have stitched it," I said to no one in particular.

"What did you say?" asked Mickey.

"I should have taken a chance and put a stitch in his lip. But I was scared." I began to cry.

Mickey took both my shoulders in his hands and he looked me in the eye. "Listen to me, young lady. You did more than most people would have. You saved those men. You can't be expected to do everything. It's not possible to do everything."

I wiped my nose with a glove. "Little girl," he said sternly, "you're braver than I am." Then he hugged me and abruptly turned away. I heard him make a muffled noise. Oh man, was he crying, too?

"He's right, Tuli," said Rowdy as he smacked his huge pink wad of gum. "You did everything I always dream about. I always wonder how I'll act if I'm in a tough spot like this. You did it beautifully. Now, go in there and eat at least half that hot apple pie that someone just brought you."

Before I ate the pie, I went over to see the lost hunters, who were now found and on their way to the hospital, then home.

"Hey, T-T-Tuli," Mr. Martin said loudly. He sat on a snowmobile wrapped in a blanket as he waited for Dr. Burnett to look at him. "You made it. I knew you would." He still had ice in his moustache. A mittened hand reached out for me. I took it.

"Yeah. And so did you. How did it go?"

"Gr-gr-great. We did what you said. We ate the f-f-food and drank a lot of water. Had to pee a lot though." He laughed at that. "We heard c-c-coyotes and got a little scared. We had our r-r-rifles though." He smiled.

I wondered what would have happened if all of them had ammo and opened up with their rifles at the same time. It's just about impossible to hit a coyote. They probably would have hit each other. Luckily, they were out of bullets.

He touched my arm. "Thanks Tuli. I mean it. I don't th-th-think we could have made it without you." He sniffed loudly. "I learned a big lesson."

"A lot of lessons," said Mr. Johnston as he sipped at a cup of steaming coffee. "I brought my son with me. I thought this would be a nice camping trip. I had no idea things could turn out like this. No idea." He looked down at the cup and thought about things he probably wouldn't tell anyone. Shame does that.

Mr. Wabash cried uncontrollably as the attendants put him in the big Snow Cat that would take them all to Jacob Lake Inn, where their families and the ambulances waited to take them on dry roads to the hospital in Page. Safely inside the Cat, Mr. Wabash saw me through the window. He waved then dropped his head onto the stretcher like a man who exhausted all his mental and physical energy.

"Time to go," Mickey said to the others. "You all are going to Jacob Lake Inn to see your families. Then you'll go to Page for a visit at the hospital. Good luck to you."

Mickey went to the Operations table. I watched him throw his walkie talkie onto the pile of maps. Then he kicked over a chair.

There's something odd about completing a search. It's exciting, but at the same time annoying. I mean, we want to find the lost people and make certain they're okay. We're also mad that they made us look for them. It's hard to explain, but I guess it's like what Mom's policeman friend says: "We're here to serve, even if it means saving a bunch of dummies who can get us hurt in the process of saving them."

I turned around to find my family standing right behind me. Dad held my big-eyed brother who was now eating a hot dog.

"Life's hard lessons." Mom said evenly. "Time to eat some more. The press is gonna be all over us when we get to Jacob Lake and you need your strength."

Tired, shaky and a bit sad, I did what she said.

Back to that plate of steaming eggs and veggies with a side of hashed browns that waited for me. Mom sat down and crossed her arms on the table. Her red, wind-burned cheeks made the dark smears under her eyes appear darker. We got home around three this morning and she probably didn't sleep much.

"Honey, you'll have to deal with the press for months. You're a hot topic right now. You saved those men and you survived a snowstorm. People find that interesting."

"Yeah," agreed Pete. "Especially the men you saved."

I stared at my plate of food.

"What if my best isn't good enough?"

"When has your best not been good enough?"

"I ruined the *kapucha* game. And I tried my best."

Mom and Dad looked at each other, but Pete spoke. "Tuli, so what? You think that all those other girls haven't messed up? I saw Arnie trip and fall twice in one game. Jen never scores. You always score. Just because you only scored once that game doesn't mean you're a loser. They depend on you."

The phone rang and Dad inspected the caller id. "New York area code," he said. He picked up the receiver. "Hello. Yes it is." He listened a few minutes and we could hear the woman on the other end talking. "No kidding? Well, give me your number and I'll have her call you. Yes, I will. Bye." He wrote the message and handed it to me.

"A Sheena Livingston. She said she met you at the Flagstaff airport."

I had to think a second. "Oh, Mom. You know. It was that woman in the weird clothes."

"And so?" Mom asked.

"She's a senior editor at Marvin Lupert Publishing. She wants to talk to Tuli about doing a book."

"On what?"

"On Tuli."

We sat in silence for a moment. I lost my appetite but only because I felt a bit confused by the attention.

The phone rang again. Once more Dad looked at the caller id. "Another New York area code," he told us.

"Go ahead and get it," Mom said.

"Hello." Dad listened for a minute. A slow smile started then he said, "I think that would be fine. Just a sec. She's right here."

"Who is it?" Mom asked.

"*New York Times.*"

"Wow," said Pete. "The big time."

"Okay," Mom answered. She's used to getting phone calls from reporters. "I'll take it in the den. Y'all finish eating."

"Uh, hon," Dad said. "It's not for you."

"No?" Mom seemed surprised.

He smiled big. "This one's for Tuli, too."

Glossary

ATV: All terrain vehicle used by hunters, mushers training their sled dogs in the off-season (with no snow) and ATV enthusiasts who like to ride across the countryside. Some are three wheeled, but the safest are four-wheeled.

CPR: Cardiopulmonary resuscitation. Artificial circulation is used when a person's heart has stopped. The heart is squeezed so that blood is forced into vessels where it can be carried to the lungs to be oxygenated and also to parts of the body. You also must artificially ventilate the person so he/she receives oxygen into the lungs. Call your local Red Cross, YMCA or activities center to inquire about CPR classes. They are not difficult or expensive and children can learn CPR.

Dehydration: You can feel that you are dehydrated when your urine is very dark, and there is not much of it. You will be very thirsty. People do not automatically drink enough water to replace the water lost through daily activities and natural processes. If you are thirsty, that means you already are on the road to dehydration.

Frostbite: The term frostbite refers to local cooling injuries. There are several types of frostbite, ranging from incipient frostbite that is also known as 'frost nip," when your ears, fingers, toes or cheeks have been exposed to cold and becomes white. If not warmed, it can turn into 'superficial frostbite' that turns the affected part white and waxy; it feels frozen to the touch. The next step is serious. 'Deep frostbite' involves the skin, fat, muscles, tendons and bones. The area turns gray and blue and feels hard. This requires serious medical attention. Do not rub with snow.

Hasty Search: Many times at the end of the day or when bad weather is about to set in, trackers do a "hasty search" without formal plan or much organization. They take off in the general direction the victims headed then they search quickly and hope that they'll be fortunate enough to find who they're looking for. Quick searches are often used when the daylight is fading and especially when it's believed the lost person is a child or might be hurt.

Hot shots: Firefighters who fight forest fires. Some are associated with the U.S. Forest Service. There are American Indian hot shots, like the Chief Mountain Hotshots, a crew based on the Blackfeet Indian Reservation in North Central Montana. The crew works out of the Blackfeet Agency B.I.A. (Bureau of Indian Affairs) office in Browning, Montana. Hot shots have a grueling, dangerous job and often they do not receive much payment for doing it.

Hypothermia: General body cooling is properly known as systemic hypothermia. The body's core temperature is 98.6 degrees F. Death usually occurs at 78 degrees F. You can become hypothermic if you are in cold, wet weather and cannot stay dry and warm. Hypothermia can develop in variety of temperatures, even from 38-50 degrees F if the person has inadequate protection from wind, rain, and water. You an also loose body heat by being in cool water, becoming exhausted in otherwise comfortable temperatures. Always wear a hat in cold weather and stay dry.

Operations Camp: The site of the search headquarters where searchers report, eat, receive orders and stay the night.

Operational Leader: The leader of the search who, on advice from his/her teams, makes decisions as to who will search and where. The Operations leader finds resources, dictates duties and expects to gather information from the searchers.

PLS: Point Last Seen. The last place the lost person or persons were seen.

Polypropylene: An important material used in glove liners and long underwear that absorbs sweat. Polypropolene keeps moisture away from your body and is a must for hikers, skiers and hunters in winter so that you don't become chilled. It does absorb sweat odors, so you must wash it after every use.

Topographic Map: Topographic map show the shape of the Earth's surface with contour lines, those imaginary lines that join sites of the same elevation on the surface of the land. These lines allow readers to learn the height of hills and mountains, in addition to the steepness of the slopes, plus depth of trenches of the ocean. A topographic map might also include symbols that show rivers, streams, woods and streets.

Trailing Dog: Ground scent and starting point are most important for a trailing dog. They work well if they have a scent article from the lost person.

Searching Dog: These dogs work more with air scents and do not need a ground scent or a scent article, although it is helpful to have one.

About the Author

Award winning author Oklahoma Choctaw Devon Mihesuah has written extensively about American Indian histories and cultures and is Professor of Applied Indigenous Studies at Northern Arizona University in Flagstaff. She also serves as Editor of the international journal of indigenous studies, the *American Indian Quarterly*. Her many books emphasize empowerment for Natives through storytelling and recovering traditional indigenous knowledge. Her books include the novels, *The Lightning Shrikes* (Lyons Press, 2004) and *The Roads of My Relations* (Arizona, 2000) in addition to the non-fiction books, *American Indigenous Women: Decolonization, Empowerment, Activism* (University of Nebraska Press, 2003); *Recovering Our Ancestors' Gardens: Indigenous Recipes and Guide to Good Health* (Nebraska, 2005) and *So You Want to Write About American Indians? A Guide for Scholars, Students and Writers* (Nebraska, 2005). She has been at one time or another a scholar, lifeguard, distance runner, Tae Kwon Do black belt, musher, skijorer, gun salesperson, cook, high school biology and physics teacher and swimming, basketball, cross country and tennis coach. She lives in Arizona with her husband Josh and children Toshaway and Ariana. Visit her website at http://jan.ucc.nau.edu/~mihesuah.

Also by Devon Mihesuah

So You Want to Write About American Indians? A Guide for Scholars, Students and Writers

Recovering Our Ancestors' Gardens: Indigenous Recipes and Guide to Good Health

American Indigenous Women: Decolonization, Empowerment, Activism

American Indians: Stereotypes and Realities

Cultivating the Rosebuds: The Education of Women at the Cherokee Female Seminary, 1851-1909

The Lightning Shrikes (fiction)

The Roads of My Relations (fiction)

Edited Works:

With Waziyatawin Angela Wilson: *Indigenizing the Academy: Transforming Scholarship and Empowering Communities*

'First To Fight': The Story of Henry Mihesuah

Repatriation Reader: Who Owns Indian Remains?

Natives and Academics: Discussions on Researching and Writing About American Indians.

Printed in the United States
81951LV00002B/1-87